FLAWLESS

A STREET LOVE TALE

JADE JONES

www.jadedpublications.com

This novel is a work of fiction. Any reference to real people, events, establishments, or locales is intended only to give the fiction a sense of reality and authenticity. Other names, characters, and incidents occurring in the work are either the product of the author's imagination or are used fictitiously, as are those fictionalized events and events that involve real persons. Any character that happens to share the name of a person who is any acquaintance of the author, past or present, is purely coincidental and is in no way intended to be an actual account involving that person.

Contact the Author

Instagram/Twitter: Jade_Jones89

Facebook: Author Jade Jones

Email: jaded_publications@yahoo.com

FLAWLESS

1

"Damn…You lookin' good, girl," Cool smiled. He pulled his fiancé, Kimberlyn Lopez into a firm hug. It felt like an eternity since the last time he'd saw her. A year behind bars felt like an entire life.

Holding onto his baby's mother, Cool relished the way her firm, curvy body melted in his embrace. Tossing the correctional officers a few extra dollars to let him touch his girl was well worth every penny; and Cool didn't miss the opportunity to squeeze her ass before they separated.

At 5"5, Kimberlyn was the closest thing to perfection. Smooth medium-beige skin, olive green eyes, and a sexy coke bottle shape she was the whole entire package and then some. Born to a Salvadoran father and African-American mother, Kim was blessed with the best of both worlds.

Long flowing jet black hair stopped inches above her round, plump booty; and the faint beauty mark on her cheek only added to her sex appeal.

Cool hated to think about his soon-to-be wife keeping time with some other nigga while he was locked up, yet she'd never given him any reason to doubt her before. Since day one, she'd been his ride or die.

Kim was only twenty when Cool scooped her up and showed her the finer things in life.

As a matter of fact, she was waiting at the bus stop when he pulled alongside her in a clean Jaguar S-type. Back then he was breaking serious bread working as second in command for a well-known drug Lord in Atlanta.

Although most women threw themselves at Cool because of who he was affiliated with, there was something about Kim that drew him to her. Truth be told, he'd circled the block many times before prior to him finally speaking. He knew her well before she knew him, so he knew just how to approach her.

Even though Cool knew she was a little out of his league, he couldn't deny his attraction to a working woman. After tossing a little game and a couple compliments her way, Kim eagerly climbed inside his ride and the rest was history.

"Speak for yourself," Kim smiled, returning to reality. She took a seat at the stainless steel table across from Cool. Same routine. Different day. "Looks like you've been getting swoll' in here."

Chuckling softly, Cool took a seat across from her. "Hell yeah. Ain't shit to do but lift in dis mufucka."

Kim studied the love of her life as he went on about his workout regimen, the inmates he'd met and took under his wing, and his plans of climbing the ranks in the drug game when—and *if*—he was released.

At 6"2, Christopher "Cool" Williams was every woman's fantasy, and every girlfriend's nightmare. With smooth caramel skin, hazel eyes and a toned physique, Cool was the typical pretty boy. The small crescent shaped scar over his left eye was her favorite imperfection about him. He was a thug by nature, and lived life as such.

Shaking her head, Kim continued to listen to him rant. You'd think a seven year stretch in a minimum security facility would evoke some common sense in Cool. But all he could do was talk about his niggas and getting back on. After several minutes of listening to her fiancé go on about the very thing that landed him in prison, Kimberlyn finally snapped.

"I drove damn near four hours to get here, Cool," she reminded him. "You'd think you could ask about your son at least once."

Cool guffawed before leaning forward. "Damn girl. You ain't give a nigga a chance," he said. Truthfully, he would've never asked if it weren't for her suggesting it. He was about as successful in the fatherhood department as he was avoiding prison. Cool had dedicated his life to the hustle. All the other shit in between was just that. "How's lil' me doin'?" he asked.

Smiling brightly, Kim went on to tell Cool that their son, Jordan was starting kindergarten in the fall. However, in mid-sentence, he rudely cut her off. "Aye, you got dat for me or what?"

Kim instantly cut her eyes at Cool in irritation. *Did this motherfucker really just interrupt me to ask about some damn drugs*?

It was obvious that Cool didn't care about her, their son, or what was happening in their lives. All he cared about was his precious reputation in the dope game.

This nigga ain't gon' never change, Kim finally told herself. *No matter how I hard I go for him, I'll always come second.*

"Do I got that for you?" Kim repeated sarcastically. "Yeah, I got it…"

Without warning, Kim stood to her feet and reached down the front of her jeans.

Cool's eyes popped open in surprise at her unexpected behavior. "AYE! What da fuck is you doin'?"

"Take yo' fuckin' dope! It's obvious that bullshit is more important than me and Jordan!" Kim said, launching an eight-ball at him.

"Aye, yo! *Chill*!" He quickly grabbed the tiny baggie off the floor before the C.O. noticed. "Calm yo' ass the hell down 'fore you get us both fucked up!"

"Fuck you," Kim retaliated.

In the blink of an eye, Cool jumped to his feet and snatched her little ass up. “I told you to chill. Don’t think four walls and a roof will stop me from fucking you up. Act like you know a nigga.”

Kimberlyn’s face was beet red from embarrassment. Looking over Cool’s shoulder, she glanced at the correctional officer who was preoccupied with a newspaper. She was sure he’d heard the disturbance, but surprisingly he hadn’t budged.

“Dat mufucka damn sure ain’t gon’ stop me,” Cool told her, apparently reading her thoughts. “Now sit yo’ ass down and act like you got some sense.”

“I don’t wanna sit down, Cool—”

“You can either sit down willingly or have me do it for you,” he said. “It’s your choice.”

Kimberlyn knew Cool better than anybody. Underestimating his threats was as foolish as walking into traffic—and just as dangerous.

Reluctantly, she took a seat at the stainless steel table. “I don’t wanna do this no more, Cool,” she said, looking down at her hands. “I’m done with this shit…All of it…”

Cool reached over and placed his hands over hers. “What’chu mean you done? We can’t afford to be throwin’ in the towel early—”

"No, *you* can't afford it," Kim reminded him. "The stocks you had me invest in before you got locked up have been booming. Me and Jordan will be good for a while—"

"And what happens if that changes? A mufucka can't sleep peacefully without having a backup plan," Cool whispered. "K, I need you to keep bringin' in this work—"

"No."

Cool quickly withdrew his hands as if Kim's skin had seared him. "No?"

"I'm done," Kim reiterated. "D-O-N-E," she spelled out.

"Hol' up. Wait a minute. What's all this?" he asked. "Where this even coming from?"

Tears pooled in Kimberlyn's eyes as she fought to control herself. From her peripheral vision she could see the other visitors looking at them strangely. She'd made a total scene, but Cool had a tendency of upsetting her publicly.

Back when he was free, it was the same sad song. Cool took Kim through hell and high water with his side chick drama and dominating ways. And in order to ensure she stayed, he spoiled her endlessly. All the designer wear she owned, and all the newest cars she pushed. Yet after Cool's imprisonment all that quickly changed.

Most of his savings went to legal fees, and Kimberlyn was left to take care of their home. Had it not been for Cool investing his drug money, she would've broke as hell. Now she was smuggling him in coke just so he could stay afloat behind prison walls. Risking her freedom was not what Kim had in mind when committing to their relationship—but she loved Cool and was willing to do whatever for him. Truthfully, he was the only one who could convince her to do such reckless shit. Unfortunately, love had a way of making people do crazy things.

Slowly standing to her feet, Kim prepared to walk away from it all—including her baby daddy. Tears continued to stream down her vanilla cheeks as she shook her head vehemently. "I thought I could be who you needed when you needed…but I can't do this shit with you."

"Hey…," Cool stood to his feet and approached Kim. Gently tilting her chin up to face him, he looked deeply into her eyes. Even in his prison scrubs, he was just as handsome as the day they'd met. As a matter of fact, it was his pretty boy looks that reeled Kim in his clutches. "I don't know where all this shit comin' from…but you gon' do this as long as I need you to. When I get on you gon' be right up at the top with me, K. That's always how it's been—and prison ain't gon' change that. Now come on," he urged. "Pull yaself together, bay. I need you to think clearly if we gon' keep doin' this shit."

Kim sniffled and wiped away her oncoming tears. Mascara mixed with eyeliner stained her cheeks. She wanted so badly to believe Cool could take care of her and Jordan…but with him being locked up, the only thing he could do was cause her to end up in the same situation. Kim knew it was time to finally grow up and put the careless shit to the side…If not for herself, for the sake of their son.

Slowly backpedaling away from Cool, it felt like she was seeing him for the first time. "I am thinking clearly," Kim whispered. "I'm sorry, Cool…"

"Kim…?"

She didn't even bother responding as she hastily left the visiting room.

"KIMBERLYN?!" she heard Cool scream after her.

Tears blurred her vision as she quickly exited the premises. Kim figured the sooner she put some distance between her and Cool the better. The minute she reached her 2013 Range Rover, she hopped inside and broke down crying hysterically.

After bawling for what felt like forever, Kimberlyn finally contained herself and started the ignition. Today's visit didn't end how she had expected, and it hurt like hell to walk away.

I hope my girl Shayla is having a better day.

2

Shayla Edwards scrolled through her Instagram timeline like she wasn't on the clock at work. Instead of making herself readily available to customers, she was seeking entertainment through social media. Truthfully, it was the only way she could keep her mind off her recent nasty break up with her ex, Dexter.

At twenty-four, Shayla was forced to move back home after discovering him in bed with another bitch—and to further add insult to injury, a white one at that. One year and three months into a relationship, Shayla didn't expect her world to come crashing down so soon.

Like every woman, she had high hopes of one day getting married. Yet instead of getting the storybook wedding she'd envisioned she got a harsh dose of reality.

Shayla was reading the latest gossip on *BallerAlert* when a smooth, deep voice spoke up from behind.

"Aye, excuse me, Miss Lady?"

The base in the stranger's tone made the hairs on the back of Shayla's neck stand. Quickly, she pocketed her iPhone and turned to face the customer awaiting her assistance.

"Sorry about that. How can I help…" Shayla's voice instantly trailed off after realizing how handsome he was. "You..."

The gorgeous specimen standing in front of her chuckled lightly, revealing the cutest set of dimples. At 6"2, he had skin the color of cinnamon and low jet black hair. From the texture alone, Shayla assumed that he had some foreign ancestry in his lineage. Wide mahogany eyes were complimented by lashes that curled upward naturally, and his lips looked damn near kissable.

Shayla's gaze quickly traveled from his perfect face down to his toned biceps. The royal blue Armour shirt he wore hugged his broad chest and outlined every muscle in his eight-pack. She also marveled at the impressive dragon tattoos that made his left arm's sleeve.

Shayla's eyes traveled lower. She could tell through his track pants that he was slightly bowlegged—a secret weakness of hers for years.

Damn, he's fine, her conscience screamed.

"So I just moved here from Cali not too long and I'm lookin' for a bed to purchase. You think you can help me with that…Shayla?" he asked, reading her nametag.

Shayla had to stop herself from staring too hard as she fought to keep her composure. The way her name rolled off his tongue made her tingle in places that shouldn't have been aroused.

"Um…I…of course," she stammered. "Let me show you our section. It's quite expansive." As soon as she turned on her heel and walked off, he stole a view of her round derrière.

For the better part of his life, Romeo had always been attracted to ratchet chicks and the entertainment that came with them. However, he couldn't deny that Shayla was attractive—even in her prescription frames.

Romeo always had a thing for chocolate girls so he was smitten at first glance. Even without a drop of makeup on, Shayla's skin was flawless. There wasn't an imperfection in site. Long bone straight treks stopped an inch or two past her bra strap, and thankfully it was all hers. Her lips were his favorite feature; plump and primed.

Shayla had the whole girl next door look going on, but Romeo knew there was much more to her than the surface.

Looking over his shoulder, Romeo glanced at his friends who were scoping out furniture to buy for themselves. A few weeks ago he'd closed the deal on a baby mansion; and even though the place came fully furnished, he couldn't settle on a pre-owned bed.

Romeo looked back over at Shayla.

A nigga like me will turn her nerdy ass out, he arrogantly thought to himself.

Once Shayla reached the furniture section, she turned to explain the different features—but caught him looking dead at her ass. Immediately, her cheeks flushed because no guy had looked at her that way since Dexter.

Girl, get it together and do your job, Shayla scolded herself. "This is our Stockholm bed—priced at $899," she continued. "It features natural materials such as solid wood and leather to ensure the bed ages beautifully."

Romeo was only halfway interested in what she was saying by then. One track-minded, he was now more concerned with drawing down on her. He'd been in Atlanta two whole days and had yet to have any real fun. As usual, business was a top priority.

"The one next to it is the Bekkestua—priced at nearly $2000. It features a beautiful button-tufted headboard and is very comfy to relax in while watching TV."

Romeo slowly made his way over towards the luxury bed. "Is that right?" he asked, taking a seat on it. Using the tips of his fingers, he pushed down on the mattress to see how sturdy it was.

Shayla tried her best not to notice the elephant imprint in his track pants. *Lord, Jesus see me through this*, she told herself.

"It comes with the mattress, right?"

Shayla literally had to tear her gaze away from the bulge in his pants to focus. “Uh—yes. Yes, it does.”

Standing to his feet, Romeo reached inside his track pants’ pocket. “Shit, run it,” he said, pulling out a thick wad of cash. “I’ll take the bed…and ya number too.”

3

Shayla was on her way back to her parent's townhome in Atlantic Station when her cellphone suddenly rang. Believing it was Romeo, she anxiously pulled her iPhone out her satchel. During the process, some fellas in a nearby Expedition honked at her as they drove by.

Damn. I need a car, Shayla thought, loathing the unwanted attention. Luckily, her parents didn't live too far from her work place; but Shayla would be lying if she said she didn't miss having a whip. Back when she and Dexter were together, they shared his BMW 3 Series. However, the minute Shayla broke things off, she lost that leisure.

Much to her surprise, it wasn't Romeo calling. It was her best friend Kimberlyn. *He didn't take me as the type to call on the first day anyway*, Shayla convinced herself.

Tucking her long hair behind her ear, she answered before the line went to voicemail. "Hello?"

"Hey, bitch. What you doing right now?" Kim playfully asked. From her end, it sounded like she was driving.

"Just leaving work. On my way back to the house," Shayla told her.

Kim glanced at the time displayed on the radio and noticed it was 6:00 p.m. *What a waste of a fucking day*, she thought.

"What about you?" Shayla asked.

"Girl, just left Jackson from seeing Cool's ass. Bitch, believe me when I say, I'm done with that nigga. I ain't accepting no calls. There will be no more visits. I'm just cool on Cool. Period."

Shayla laughed as she headed to the front door of her townhome. Her fifty-two year old father was mowing the lawn while soaking up the sun on that beautiful day. Had he not been so physically fit, Shayla would've been worried. But her father was a proud man who firmly believed there was no such thing as being 'too old'.

"Girl, you say that every other month," Shayla reminded Kim while waving to her father. "I mean, hell, you were the one telling me it wasn't gonna be easy holding your man down in prison. What changed now?"

"That's just it. *Change*," Kim emphasized. "That nigga ain't gon' *never* change. I ain't got time for it no more, Shay."

Shayla walked inside her home and immediately headed to her bedroom for some privacy. Now that she was living with her parents again, it seemingly came rarely. "You knew that already," Shayla told her friend.

For years Shayla had watched Cool drag Kimberlyn through hell and high water. And still, she stayed—even with all the late night creeping, side chicks, and physical and verbal abuse. Truth be told, Shayla had never cared for Kim's fiancee, but she did respect his place in her life.

"Ugh, I did. But I still believed there was hope," Kim said. "But fuck all that. I'm trying to get out and do something tonight. Need to take my mind off the B.S. with him. You down?"

Shayla kicked her off sneakers and plopped down on her full size mattress. It was a huge step down from the California king size canopy she once slept in with Dex. Yet it was also a valuable lesson when it came to rushing into some shit. After all, she and Dexter had only been dating three months before they hastily decided to move in together.

Shayla blew out a long dramatic breath as she deliberated on her answer. "Girl, you know I don't do that club shit."

"Grandma, you don't do *shit* but sell Ikea," Kim joked. "That's why you need to come up out that house and kick it. Just me and you."

Shayla instantly perked up after hearing Kim's friend, Nina wouldn't be joining them. She liked her about as much as she liked Cool—which was virtually nonexistent. Though the two had never exchanged words, Shayla just didn't care for Nina's ratchet persona. She was loud, obnoxious, and an attention whore by nature.

"*Hmm*…I guess…," Shayla finally said after carefully considering it.

"Bet! I'll be there around ten."

4

Don't know why I came in this club with you, girl...

Don't know why I came in with these diamonds on my chain...

Surrounded by bad bitches I can't get 'em out my face...

Maybe 'cuz a nigga handsome and wealthy...

Is it 'cuz a nigga cook like a professor...?

I don't know how you feel can you tell me...

I won't know how you feel 'til you tell me...

Is it 'cuz a nigga handsome and wealthy...?

Romeo and his boy Desmond held shit down from the VIP section like the young bosses they were. Popping champagne bottles, and smoking the finest skunk they were mistakenly assumed to be local celebrities.

The small section was crowded with a plethora of beautiful women from every shade and nationality. There were enough females for every nigga in VIP to have three—and that was only if Romeo was willing to share.

Drawing the most attention to himself, the young show boater was draped in several expensive yellow canary diamond chains. A $720 Vivienne Westwood button down hugged his chiseled torso. Black designer jeans hung casually off his waist, and on his size twelve feet was a pair of matte black Giuseppes.

Two beautiful women sat on either side of him, each vying for a place in his life—no matter how insignificant. Sexy, wealthy and new to the city, Romeo was fresh meat to the vultures looking for a baller. And even though he knew their motives, Romeo still loved the attention. Twenty-five without a care in the world, he didn't plan on settling down anytime soon.

Much like his homie, Desmond Wright was also quite the exhibitionist. Sporting a crisp white V-neck, white jeans, and white and black python high tops, he oozed a million dollars. Around his tattooed neck was over two hundred grand in jewelry easily, and his wrist sparkled with a new shiny Rolex.

Entrepreneurs in their own right, Romeo and Desmond loved to flaunt their wealth. Born and raised in poverty, it felt good to wake up every morning without a financial care in the world.

Growing up, all they'd ever known was the grisly streets of Compton. Banging and selling drugs was their life until they finally made a come up some four years ago; one that changed their lives forever.

Pink Dragon was currently the hottest marijuana on the market. Frosted in a fuchsia-colored substance, it contained one of the strongest strains known to man. Rappers talked about it in their songs, and all the A-listers back in Hollywood were familiar.

Media quickly labeled their weed as the most potent, and just like that Romeo and Desmond became overnight celebrities. However, they couldn't take all the credit for their speedy rise to success. Truth be told, their achievement wouldn't even be possible if it wasn't for Ava—the third wheel in the trio.

Posted next to Desmond in a black Herve Leger dress, no one would've ever thought Ava would be mixed in with such a business. Half-Alaskan and half-Polynesian, the 5"6 bombshell was breathtaking at first glance.

Long, wavy jet black hair flowed freely down Ava's back and stopped just inches above her curvy ass. Her tight, slanted eyes were hazel, and she had the cutest pair of dimples. Her athletic body and pretty smile were just the added bonuses.

Though Ava had the whole package—money, intelligence, and good looks, her love life was deplorable. Since a teenager, she'd always had a poor sense of judgment when it came to men—and because of that she rarely dated nowadays.

It was a man who'd convinced her to move to the states in the first place. Kent Summers—a wealthy real estate tycoon—had promised Ava the world and more after swearing to divorce his wife of ten years.

He'd met the exotic beauty while on vacation, and just couldn't ignore his attraction. In the beginning, Kent spoiled with her luxuries, and talked a good game. But like they say; if something seems too good to be true it probably is.

Ava dropped everything to move to Hollywood to be with him. Yet when she got there it was a whole other story. Apparently, Kent was in too deep since his wife hadn't signed a prenuptial. The last thing he wanted to do was give away half his estate so he stayed begrudgingly, breaking Ava's heart in the process.

On her own with nothing but a Visa waiver, Ava hotel-hopped until the day she met Romeo and Desmond. At the time, they'd been trying their hardest to develop a strain so potent it put white widow to shame. Ironically, Ava had majored in botany, and the rest was history.

Unlike Romeo and Desmond, Ava didn't look like she was having anywhere near as much fun. Truthfully, she didn't care for the large crowds, but she knew keeping up their image was important—especially in their profession. Besides, they'd just moved to Atlanta from L.A. two days ago so naturally they wanted to see what the night life was hitting on.

An increase in demand had led the trio to the Peach State to begin with. Although Romeo and Desmond loved relocating, Ava could take it or leave it. ATL wasn't really her cup of tea. She missed the beaches and the smell of saltwater. But instead of pouting about it, she rolled with the punches for the sake of a paycheck.

Twelve people deep, Romeo and Desmond's camp was relatively small, but they didn't mind. In the words of Jay-Z, 'less was more'. In a game where greed could make the most loyal person turn, they could only afford to fuck with their day-ones.

The small posse was the rowdiest in the club, yet management wouldn't dare put a stop to it—especially not after Romeo had bought out the entire bar. As usual, money spoke volumes.

Meanwhile downstairs, Kimberlyn and Shayla shuffled through the thick crowd of club-goers in an attempt to find an empty space. *Compound* was overly packed that evening for the Atlanta Falcons after party. But surprisingly, it wasn't their section that was garnering the most attention that night. The two Cali boys undoubtedly had the place on lock.

In the midst of heading towards the bar, Kim looked over at the noisy VIP section. Pungent smoke clouds hung in the air, bottles were popping, and everybody looked like they were having a good old time.

“Hold up,” Kimberlyn said, stopping dead in her tracks. “Is that…Nah, it can’t be…”

Shayla was so caught off guard by her friend’s abrupt stop that she bumped into the back of her. Luckily, she had impeccable balance in her six-inch heels. “What? Who is it?” Shayla asked, clearly confused.

Kimberlyn didn’t even bother responding as she grabbed Shayla’s hand and headed over to VIP.

5

“Wait, where are we going?” Shayla asked.

The moment she saw Romeo, she felt a faint flush of color rise in her face. Naturally, Shayla wasn’t all too pleased with the sight of him surrounded by beautiful women. *So that’s why he didn’t hit me up…*If her pride wasn’t wounded before, it certainly was now.

Shayla tried her best to hold onto her confidence, especially after it was diminished by Dexter. But she’d be lying to herself if she said she wasn’t a little bit bothered. *This is why I never get my hopes too high when it comes to dating.*

“I don’t feel like going over there,” Shayla said.

Irritated by her friend’s usual ‘stick-in-the-mud’ personality, Kim turned on her heel and faced Shayla. “And why not?” she asked, hands on hips.

Shayla didn’t feel comfortable telling Kim it was because of Romeo, so she blamed it on something else. “It’s already too many chicks over there…”

Kimberlyn burst out laughing hysterically. “Bitch, them insignificant ass hoes ain’t got shit on us!” she said. “Please don’t tell me that’s the issue. Because it’s *certainly* not for me.”

Had Kim brought her girl Nina instead of Shayla, she would never be having that conversation. Nina was down for whatever whereas Shayla was timid when it came to certain shit. However, Kim was determined to break her out of that. *Damn, Shay could be such a bore sometimes.*

"Come on. You tripping," Kim said, leading a reluctant Shayla to the VIP.

Ever the passive type, Shayla hesitantly followed behind her friend.

Kim was right about one thing though. The moment they barged into the paid-for section, all attention immediately went to them. Shayla's stomach flip-flopped nervously as she tried her best to cover her exposed bosom. She felt extremely underdressed in the pink cutout dress Kim had brought for her to wear.

I don't know why I let this broad talk me into coming here, Shayla thought.

Kimberlyn looked overly provocative in a pair of skin tight leather shorts and a denim bustier. Apparently, she was trying to fuck up Cool's name and rep after their "split." With her size D's spilling over, it was obvious that she was looking to get the attention of every man in the place. Cool would have a fit if he wasn't locked up. He'd never permitted her to dress that way and Kim knew it. Shayla, on the other hand, was a bit more modest.

Kimberlyn had no qualms about interrupting a conversation with a random groupie. "Desmond?" she asked, somewhat in disbelief. For a second, she thought her eyes were deceiving her.

The ghetto bird he was speaking with instantly rolled her eyes in disgust. She'd been trying to snag the baller all night before Kim showed up unwelcomed. *Cheap bitch*, she thought, eyeing Kimberlyn's tasteless outfit. She wasn't wearing anything designer, and yet she had the audacity to barge in their VIP.

"Kimberlyn…?" Desmond said, equally taken back. "Damn, is that you?"

"My, my, my. What a coincidence running into you tonight."

Shayla looked from Desmond to Kimberlyn and instantly wondered about their history. Kim had never mentioned him in the three years they'd been friends.

"Damn, girl. Shit, how long has it been?" Desmond asked, walking over to her.

"Too long," Kimberlyn said, leaning in for a hug.

Desmond wrapped his strong arms around Kimberlyn and held her tightly. His expensive cologne surrounded the two women, and his sex appeal was undeniable. Even Shayla had to keep from staring a bit too hard.

Caramel complexion, mahogany-colored eyes, and an athletic build, Desmond was the epitome of a pretty boy who was slightly rough around the edges. Between him and Romeo, Desmond was certainly the level-headed one.

Years ago, before he and Romeo made their come up, they had visited Atlanta with a few friends. It was then that Desmond met Kimberlyn while she was dancing at *Blue Flame*. The two hit it off instantly, and Desmond even delayed his flight an extra two weeks. Yet all good things eventually come to an end. With a two-year old daughter back home, Desmond had no choice but to return to the real world. Reluctantly, he went back to Cali to be with his baby mama, and Kimberlyn went on to meet Cool.

Although Desmond and Kim's rendezvous only lasted a few weeks, she still held a special place in his heart, and vice-versa.

After embracing each other for what felt like an eternity, Desmond finally pulled apart and looked Kim over "You just as untouchable as I remember," he complimented.

That immediately caused Kimberlyn to blush.

Behind him, Ava shuffled in her seat as if she was uncomfortable, but no one seemed to notice.

Mona—the female Desmond was previously entertaining—didn't find anything flattering about his comment. As a matter of fact, she was quite offended. "Are you kidding me?" Mona finally spoke up. "*Untouchable*?" she snorted. "Nigga, your standards must not be that high…"

Offended by the rude remark, Kimberlyn advanced on the chick, ready to rumble. "Hold up, bitch. You obviously don't know me, but you can get to *real* quick," she threatened.

Jumping to her feet, Mona unflinchingly welcomed the challenge. "Show me, hoe!" she spat.

Desmond quickly stood between both women to keep them from clawing each other's eyes out. Moments like those occurred in his life all too frequently, but he knew just how to deal with it.

"Aye, Monte, get this loudmouth bitch up outta here, homie."

Before Mona could oppose, Romeo and Desmond's 6"5 enforcer grabbed her by the arm. "Don't touch me!" she snapped, snatching away. "I can leave by myself. I don't need help." Grabbing her clutch off the nearby leather sofa, she quickly left the VIP section—but not before flipping off Desmond.

"*Anyway*…I see you still attracted to the same type of bitches," Kimberlyn laughed. "Loud and crazy. And speaking of bitches how's your baby mama?"

Desmond gave her the side eye before plopping down on the sofa. In front of him was a table filled with a variety of bottles and champagnes for the ladies "Shit, same. Loud and crazy," he laughed. "We ain't rockin' like that no more…"

"Is *that* right?" Kim asked, joining him. She then helped herself to a glass of champagne.

Desmond couldn't help but to admire her boldness. Honestly, it was one of his favorite qualities about her.

Halfway across the club, Mona rushed over to the bar where three fellas patiently awaited her arrival. Unbeknownst to Romeo and Desmond, she had been sent over to scout them out. The game she was running was simply a front. In the end, Mona planned on making sure their asses suffered for the way they treated her.

"What it's lookin' like over there?" the leader of the trio asked once she reached him.

"It's looking like those motherfuckers need to be dealt with early!" Mona vented. "If it's one thing I hate, it's an obnoxious ass nigga."

Cackling, the leader handed her a small amount of cash for her services. They'd been running the same scheme together for years on unsuspecting cats. "Patience. All in due time," he told Mona. "All in due time…"

Meanwhile, back in VIP, Romeo couldn't stop gawking at Shayla. This time around she didn't have her glasses on, and she looked stunning in her club wear.

Damn, she bad as hell, Romeo thought to himself.

Even though he'd gotten her number earlier, he had no real intentions on ever using it. Sometimes he did shit just to know he could—like getting the digits. Truth be told, Shayla seemed like too much of a square for his standards. And judging from her standoffish attitude, he could see he wasn't too far off.

Feeling as though Romeo was giving too much attention to Shayla, the female to his right quickly stood to her feet and left. She figured she was way too classy to be kicked out like her predecessor, so she departed quietly and willingly.

Romeo didn't even bother stopping her as he continued to stare down Shayla. She was trying her hardest to pretend she didn't see him as she stood next to Kimberlyn. He actually found her demeanor to be quite cute.

Normally, Romeo didn't go for the good girl type, but there was something about Shayla that drew him to her.

The minute they finally made eye contact, Romeo beckoned her to join him.

Standing idly by—while looking extremely out of place—Shayla deliberated on whether or not she should. She already wasn't feeling the groupies surrounding him. And she'd never been one to fight for attention…or over a man for that matter.

Quit playing. You know you want to, her conscience whispered.

Pushing her pride to the side, Shayla slowly made her way over towards him and sat down. Almost instantly the tension in the air thickened between the competitions.

"What's up with you? Why you standin' there lookin' all mean and shit? I know that ain't you," Romeo said, playfully nudging her.

Shayla shrugged her shoulders, too nervous to make eye contact. "Clubs aren't really my scene," she told him.

"Oh yeah?" Romeo's eyes shifted from her pretty face down to her thick chocolate legs. He didn't see how a woman so gorgeous could be so timid. But Romeo was determined to break her out of her shell. "Well, loosen up a bit. Have a drink, and lemme help make it ya scene."

In silence, Shayla watched as he poured her a generous shot of vodka. If she didn't know any better she'd think he was purposely trying to get her loose. *If I tell him I don't drink, he's probably gonna think I'm whack*, she thought.

Keeping that bit of info to herself, Shayla hesitantly accepted the drink.

"Those shoes on fleek, boo," Ava said, peeping her heel game. Unlike the rest of the herd, she was openly friendly to Shayla. Kimberly, on the other hand, she could care less for.

"Thanks," Shayla muttered, taking a tiny sip of her beverage. The Giuseppes on her feet were two years old and a gift from Dexter. Had it not been for their value, they would've gone in the trash like most of the other things he'd gotten her.

At that point, Shayla had Romeo's undivided attention. With liquor, marijuana, and a half a pill coursing through his veins, he was definitely on one that evening.

Eyes glassy and intentions set, Romeo leaned close to Shayla's ear. "What'chu gettin' into after you leave here?" he asked.

Romeo's warm, liquor-scented breath caused the tiny hairs on the back of Shayla's neck to stand. *Damn, why does he have to be so irresistible*, she asked herself.

"Not sure. I guess whatever my girl decides. I'm riding with her," Shayla explained.

"Shit, it looks like ol' girl preoccupied with my boy," Romeo said. "You may as well slide with me. I'll take you wherever you gotta go in da mornin'."

"Um…I don't know…," Shayla hesitated. As usual, her guard was up, but for good enough reason.

"What'chu mean you don't know?" Romeo asked, somewhat offended that she was playing hard to get. In his world, bitches came as frequently as the money so he'd never had difficulty getting laid.

This chick trippin', he thought to himself. *Hell, I got three bad ass bitches waiting to do whatever the kid asks. And this chick's giving me the third degree like I'm some bum ass nigga.*

"I just don't know," Shayla said, finally turning to face him. "I barely know you."

"Hell, we can *get* to know each other. Right after we christen that new bed," he added.

"Excuse me?" Shayla asked in disgust. She totally wasn't expecting Romeo's forwardness, and it was a complete turn off. *What a fucking pig*.

Before he could respond, Shayla quickly stood to her feet and walked off.

"Where you going, Shay?" Kim called out after her.

Shayla ignored her friend as she headed towards the exit. *This is why I don't fuck with these scenes*, she thought. *Every nigga in Atlanta feels like he's entitled to talk and treat women however they want just because they're the minority. Damn that.*

Shayla didn't even bother looking behind her to see if Kim was following. All she wanted to do was put as much distance as she could between her and Romeo.

Just as Shayla was walking out, one of the doormen quickly stopped her. "Aye, hold on, baby girl. You can't go outside with that."

Shayla looked down and realized she was holding the shot glass Romeo had given her. Without hesitation, she downed the liquor before passing the glass to the doorman. He had no opposition as he stepped to the side, allowing her to leave.

Once outside, Shayla ran a hand through her wand curled hair. That night was her first time hitting the club scene since her breakup with Dexter. Unfortunately, her evening didn't end anywhere near how she imagined.

Shayla lived a pretty contained life. Coming from an upper-middleclass family, she'd been spoiled and sheltered most of her life. Oftentimes Kimberlyn even teased her by calling her grandma, but she didn't mind.

All of a sudden, Shayla regretted her choice to down the liquor. Because she didn't drink, she felt the effects almost immediately. Trying her best to keep from stumbling in her heels, she looked out for a cab but didn't see one.

Though she was only five minutes from Midtown, the last thing Shayla wanted to do was hike on foot in her Giuseppes. *Where the hell is Kimberlyn*, she wondered. A part of her was certain her best friend would come running to see what was up but apparently not.

Obviously, that nigga has her undivided attention, Shayla concluded. It usually wasn't like Kim to put a guy over her friends. However, Desmond wasn't just *any* guy.

A tiny sliver of discouragement crept into Shayla's heart before she heard a familiar voice behind her.

"Why you walk out like dat?"

As soon as she turned around, Shayla frowned at the unwanted sight of Romeo. She half-expected to see Kimberlyn, and her hopes were instantly crushed.

"Why do you think?" Shayla snapped. "Excuse my French but you're a real asshole. It's obvious you don't know how to talk to or treat women."

Romeo didn't respond immediately. *Maybe she's right.*

For the majority of his life he was used to dealing with hoes, groupies, and gold diggers. He'd never been in a seriously committed relationship before and had no real aspirations on doing so.

Women threw themselves at Romeo on a daily basis, and because of that he spoke to and treated them however he pleased. None had ever checked him about his doggish ways; none except Shayla.

"You may be right," Romeo said, taking slow steps towards her. "That shit back in there…Blame it on the liquor. Not on my heart," he told her. "If you knew me, you'd see I'm a cool ass dude. Dat ain't me."

Shayla didn't respond as she stared at him through narrowed eyes. On the low, she was impressed that he'd gone after her but she still couldn't trust him.

"Look, lemme make it up to you," Romeo offered. The look on his handsome face was genuine, but she was apprehensive when it came to him. A first impression was certainly a lasting impression.

Shayla didn't bother replying as she looked over his shoulder towards the entrance.

"Ya girl ain't comin'," Romeo said, knowing exactly who she was looking for. "I told you, she keepin' company with my homie. And it don't look like she leavin' anytime soon."

Growing cold from the breeze, Shayla hugged herself to keep warm.

"Look, you ain't gotta forgive me for that bullshit I said in there. But at least lemme take you home," he offered. "It's too damn cold out here to be standin' around."

Shayla grimaced as she weighed her options. They were definitely slim under such circumstances. "Fine," she agreed, realizing she had no other choice.

"Cool."

Putting her reservations to the side, Shayla waited for valet to pull up his whip. She literally had to keep her mouth from dropping open after a silver 2015 Porsche Spyder arrived. *Seriously*? *This is what he's pushing*?

The valet attendant anxiously hopped out before opening the passenger door for Shayla. Secretly, she relished the envious stares from chicks that were still waiting in line. The moment she climbed in, the pungent scent of marijuana filled her nostrils.

Shayla had no idea she was now playing with fire...

Focused on their own little altercation, the two of them failed to realize they were being closely watched. Parked several feet away in a black boxed Chevy were the same three goons from the bar behind tinted windows. The jack boys had been scrutinizing Romeo and Desmond all night. As soon as they noticed one leave, they hastily made their departure as well.

"You really think dem niggas brick thuggin' though?" Kevin, the youngest of the trio asked. At only eighteen, he'd abandoned his education for a life of crime with his older brother.

With wild, shoulder length dreads that were always unkempt, Kevin looked a lot like Chi town rapper, Chief Keef—and was equally as rebellious.

"Fuck you think? Look what dat nigga pushin'," Kaniel told his younger sibling. He too had dreads, but his touched the middle of his back.

"I may have to swipe that bitch too," their friend Lamar added in. He was a coffee brown brother with a face full of tattoos.

"The car or the chick?" Kaniel asked.

"Shit, both," Lamar cackled.

Together they watched as Romeo and Shayla pulled off into traffic. Keeping their distance, they followed closely behind. When it was all said and done, they knew this would be their biggest lick yet.

6

By the time Romeo pulled up to Shayla's townhome, she was slightly inebriated. Thankfully, Romeo's buzz was long gone as he eased into her driveway. "You good, babe?" he asked, turning to face Shayla.

Laughing girlishly, it was obvious she was somewhat tipsy. "Hardly," she snickered.

Climbing out, Romeo didn't notice the light that came on upstairs. He quickly rounded the car to open Shayla's door and helped her out. *Damn, she a lightweight*, he thought.

"You straight?" Romeo asked again, placing her arm around his shoulder for support.

"*Romeo*…Where 'fore art thou, Romeo?" Shayla drunkenly sang.

Suddenly, the neighbor's dog began barking at her loud antics. Shayla was too loose, but Romeo wasn't with taking advantage of chicks. That definitely wasn't his steelo.

Just as Romeo was making his way towards the house, the front door swung open. Standing there in a maroon silk robe was Shayla's mother, Tina. The disapproving look on her face instantly made Romeo feel uncomfortable but he pushed through it anyway. Besides, she wouldn't be the first mom who disliked him.

Tina Edwards was a spitting image of her daughter minus the youthfulness—but she was still beautiful nonetheless.

"Oh, Lord," Tina said, shaking her head. She knew from first glance that her daughter was drunk. "Come here, girl," she said, practically grabbing her from Romeo.

"My bad. I didn't know she had such a low tolerance," he admitted.

"Thank you for bringing her home," Tina said smugly.

"No pr—"

SLAM!

Tina rudely closed the front door in Romeo's face without so much as a goodbye. From his jewelry to his image, he stood for nothing but trouble in her eyes. It wasn't like Shayla to come home late drunk, and Tina blamed Romeo wholeheartedly.

Skipping down the stone steps, Romeo swaggered to his car. *I can tell I'ma have my hands full with that one*.

Just as he was heading to his Porsche, Romeo noticed a suspicious car creeping up the street. Almost instantly, he reached for the small piece in his waistband. He didn't leave home without it. Playing with a million dollar company there was always some nigga in the shadows gunning for his position. And not even a change of setting could change that.

Holding onto his chrome tool, Romeo watched as the boxed Chevy crept up the street. The windows were tinted so dark he was barely able to make out the shadows behind them. Romeo's heart beat in anticipation as he waited for them to make their move.

SSCRRRRRR!

The Chevy finally peeled off, leaving behind a thick gust of smoke and uneasy feeling in the pit of Romeo's stomach.

***

Thirty-two year old Dana Brooks had just popped the cork to a bottle of Hennessey when her girl Monica tapped her. The two of them were showing out and turning up with a group of niggas they'd just met at a sushi bar in L.A. After dinner and drinks, they all rolled out together to enjoy the California nightlife.

Unlike most women her age, Dana embraced the raucous lifestyle—even with an eight year old daughter.

"Bitch, tell me why yo' baby daddy on Instagram showin' off his new sidepiece?!" Monica exclaimed. With her boisterous ways, she too was a wild card and lived for the drama. However, what she didn't know was that Dana and Desmond were long over.

Dana, a habitual liar by nature, refused to let anyone know she'd been dumped six months ago. She figured it was easier holding onto hope than holding onto memories. She and Desmond had been fucking with each other way too long to admit their run was over—and in her mind it definitely wasn't.

Snatching Monica's cellphone out her hands, Dana scanned the filtered picture on her timeline. Sure enough, Desmond was booed up with some foreign-looking chick in what looked like a club. The photo was captioned: *Look who I ran into at #Compound? #CouldBeBae #WhoSaidYouCantFindLoveInTheClub*

Dana's cheeks flushed bright red after reading his comment. Angry would've been an understatement. To her knowledge, Desmond wasn't dating anybody; so to see him kicked back with some random took her by surprise—especially after she'd personally ran the last several off. Dana figured if she couldn't have Desmond no one could.

"Oh hell nah," she said. "This nigga got me all types of fucked up."

"Why you trippin', ma? You wit' me right now. Fuck dat dude," her date said. His pride was somewhat wounded after seeing Dana sweat her baby's father.

“Nigga, all you did was feed me. Don’t get ahead of your fucking self,” she snapped. “This shit right here, you don’t know nothing about.” Standing to her feet, Dana prepared to leave without even telling her guests goodbye.

“Wait, where you goin’?” Monica called after her.

“Home!”

“I thought we was hittin’ the strip club after. What you going home for?”

“Fuck you think?” Dana sassed. “To pack.”

Desmond had another thing coming if he thought she was going to let another woman steal him. A flight to Atlanta was only four hours away, and her baby daddy was in for a rude awakening.

7

"So…this is how you livin' now, huh?" Kimberlyn asked, looking around Desmond's luxury Buckhead home. After leaving *Compound*, he treated her to breakfast at *Metro Café Diner* before heading back to his crib for a nightcap. He always did know how to treat a woman.

Desmond's beautiful five-bedroom Mediterranean style mini-mansion sat on half an acre of land, and was virtually tucked off from the rest of the world. "Somebody done hit the lottery or something," she teased.

Kimberlyn didn't even feel right walking through his home with her shoes on. Everything was so shiny and brand new. *Damn, even Cool wasn't doing it this big when he was on.*

"Somethin' like that," Desmond chuckled, pulling off his $2400 biker jacket. He was fresher than the Prince of Bel-Air.

Instead of probing further, Kimberlyn eagerly walked from one room to the next. Desmond's home was truly a sight to behold, and it was obvious that he'd come up on a lil' bread since their last encounter.

"You have a beautiful place," she called out from a room in the back. "I can't believe you live here by yourself."

“Hell yeah. I worked for it.”

“What’s in here?” Kimberlyn asked, preparing to open a set of French doors.

“Oh! Whoa! Whoa! Whoa!” Desmond quickly rushed towards Kim to keep her from opening the doors. Inside was an elaborate hydroponic system, used to store and grow marijuana. The windows were blacked out so guests couldn’t see inside. There was also an intricate venting system to keep the smells under control. “Nah, don’t go in there,” he told her.

“Why not?” Kimberlyn asked, propping her hands on her wide hips. Ever the Taurus, she despised being challenged.

Placing a hand on the small of her back, Desmond slowly guided her away from the room. “’Cuz it’s not finished,” he lied. “Paint fumes might fuck with ya head.”

Kimberlyn gave him the side eye, but decided to drop it.

“Aye, you wanna drink?”

“Sure.” Kimberlyn followed Desmond inside his expansive kitchen. Beautiful cream cabinetry and sleek stainless steel appliances made the place look bright and ultra-modern. “Boy, you hardly know how to throw down. What’chu gon’ do with all this?” she teased, taking a seat on a barstool.

Opening a nearby cabinet, Desmond pulled out a five-year old bottle of Charles Heidsieck champagne. “That’s why I need you here,” he said. “A good ole’ Southern girl to take care of a West coast nigga.”

“Last I checked you had your baby mama for that,” Kimberlyn reminded him.

“Man, what’s up with you mentionin’ my baby moms all night?” he asked, slightly irritated. “I don’t see Dana anywhere ‘round this mufucka. I left her and all dat bullshit back in Cali. And I don’t need you remindin’ me about her every few hours. Feel me? Leave the past in the past.”

There was no trace of humor on Desmond’s face as he spoke. Dana Brooks had taken him through hell and high water throughout their seven year on-again-off-again-relationship. Now that he was finally free, he refused to deal with any woman’s bullshit. He’d cut a chick loose before he allowed that shit to happen again.

Breaking Dana off a cool twenty grand a month, she lived a luxurious life in Beverly Hills with their daughter—and was pretty much set for life. Every now and then, she hit Desmond up trying to rekindle what they once had, but he wasn’t trying to hear it. A young nigga was finally living stress and drama free, and he planned on keeping it that way.

"Okay…I got you," Kim said, pretending to zip her lips together. Her mouth always did get her into trouble.

Pleased with her response, Desmond poured them each a generous amount of champagne.

"I know that ain't the bottle you bought the last night you were here," Kim said. She was shocked that he'd had yet to open it. They were supposed to share it together, but never got around to it, due to the timing.

"It is," Desmond smiled.

"Why haven't you opened it yet?!" Kim asked in disbelief.

Desmond chuckled as he handed her the glass. "You wouldn't 'een believe me if I told you."

His comment left her mind wandering, but she refused to further pry. After handing her a glass, Desmond took her hand in his and led her out the kitchen.

Kimberlyn felt like she was experiencing déjà vu as she allowed him to guide her to the family room. Being with him at that very moment felt surreal. Truthfully, she hadn't even thought about Cool once since reuniting with Desmond.

Once inside, he motioned for Kimberlyn to have a seat.

Kicking her heels off, she made herself comfortable on his ivory tufted sofa. Instead of joining her, Desmond headed over to the media center. In silence, Kimberlyn watched as he activated his hi-tech Swarovski LHD fireplace. Afterwards, he placed his iPhone on the dock and turned on Pandora to set the mood.

You lift my heart up when the rest of me is down...

You, you enchant me even when you're not around...

If there are boundaries, I will try to knock them down...

I'm latching on, babe, now I know what I have found...

Disclosure's "*Latch*" poured through the speakers, causing Kim to subconsciously bob her head to the beat. After setting the mood just right, Desmond joined her on the expensive sofa. For several seconds, he simply stared at Kimberlyn in admiration. He had no idea that when he moved to Georgia, they'd bump into each other coincidentally. And now that, Kim was back in his life under different circumstances, he didn't plan on letting her go anytime soon.

Since Desmond had been in town, he'd met a few chicks out and about. But all those hoes would get sent to voicemail if that meant spending more time with Kimberlyn. She wouldn't even believe him if he told her he'd had yet to meet a chick that could compare.

Although the females came and went, none was as cool and down to earth as Kim. She was pretty, fun, and had a great sense of humor. Not to mention, she put it on a nigga when it came to intimacy. Desmond would never forget that.

"What?" Kim giggled. She felt odd with him staring at her like she was a morsel. "What's on your mind?"

Desmond slowly reached over and caressed her chin. "Nothin' much…It's just…You way prettier than I remembered."

"Boy, stop," she blushed.

"I'm dead ass, Kit-Kat."

Desmond was the only one who called her by that nickname, and she'd be lying if she said she didn't miss it.

"Come here…"

Simultaneously, they slowly leaned in close for a kiss. Kim's plush lips were just as soft as Desmond remembered. Spreading her lips with his tongue, he explored her mouth, nibbling on her bottom lip in the process. He was so gentle and passionate when it came to being intimate—the total opposite of Cool.

Suddenly, Kim pulled back after thoughts of her baby daddy crept into her mind. There was a part of her that felt guilty, but thankfully Desmond didn't notice. As a matter of fact, he had no clue about Kim's baby daddy or the fact that she had a child. She'd kept that bit of info to herself, and for good reason.

"Let's make a toast," Desmond suggested, holding up his glass.

Kimberlyn smiled. "To what?" she asked.

"Us…and new beginnings," he added.

Kimberlyn encased her bottom lip between her teeth. She liked the way it sounded, but there were so many things about her past that he didn't know. Pushing those thoughts to the side for now, Kim gently clinked her glass against his.

Together, they took a diminutive sip before Desmond placed his flute on the coffee table. Without warning, he pulled Kim on top of him, causing her to accidentally slosh some of her drink on his shirt.

That seemed to be the least of Desmond's worries as he explored her body with his large hands. She'd filled out something crazy since the last time they were together. Kim's hips had spread, her breasts were a size bigger, and her ass was off the Richter. But as soon as Desmond reached it, she quickly stopped him.

"Hold on, Dez. I gotta tell you something," Kim whispered.

Her conscience was saying one thing, but her body was saying another. She wanted Desmond badly, but she also felt guilty being with someone other than Cool. For several years, he'd been the center of her universe, doing whatever it took to provide for her and their family.

He might not be fiancé of the year, but he deserves better than this...

"What'chu gotta tell me?" Desmond asked, pinching an erect nipple through her top.

"I...I have someone in my life...," Kimberlyn finally admitted.

Desmond didn't respond right away as he stared deep into her almond-shaped eyes. He wasn't all too impressed with that realization. "What that got to do with us? You with me right now so he can't be dat significant."

Shaking her head, Kimberlyn slowly climbed off Desmond. She knew she'd picked a fine time to have regrets, but her conscience wouldn't allow her to cheat guiltlessly. "You're wrong," Kim said, holding up her ring finger. "We're engaged..."

Silence.

Honestly, it was Desmond's first time seeing the shiny rock on her finger. Up until now, he'd assumed Kimberlyn was open game. But as they say 'never assume the obvious is true.'

There was enough tension in the air to slice a knife through as they sat in total silence. Desmond never believed in stepping on another man's toes for a chick…then again, Kimberlyn wasn't just any chick.

Shaking his head, Desmond chuckled lightly. "You really know how to spring some shit up on a mufucka."

"I always did have the worst timing…"

There was another brief period of silence before Desmond responded. "You love dude?"

Kimberlyn didn't miss a beat. "Of course."

"You *in* love with him?"

Kimberlyn didn't answer so fast that go round. In fact, she had to mull over the question which spoke a thousand volumes.

After ten seconds of utter silence, Desmond took her response for what it was. Reaching for her left hand, he carefully slipped the engagement ring off her finger and placed it on the coffee table.

"I can look at you and tell you ain't fulfilled." Desmond placed a delicate kiss on the back of her hand. "You might be kickin' dat marriage shit now…but we got history," he told her.

"It's not a coincidence runnin' into each other tonight."

"I know it's not," Kim whispered.

"You oughta fuck with a real nigga, K," Desmond told her. "Leave dem lame ass niggas where you found 'em."

"I missed you," she confessed. "I'm not even gon' flex, I thought about you from time to time…"

Desmond slowly stood to his feet before helping Kim to hers. "Well, hell, it ain't nothin' like the present," he said. Taking her hand in his, Desmond led her to his massive bedroom.

Once inside, he carefully placed her on the lavish king-sized platform bed. Desmond had dropped over four grand on the high-end piece of furniture, and Kimberlyn was the first to ever grace it with her presence.

Keeping his gaze locked intently on hers, Desmond gently climbed on top of her.

"I don't want either of us to get hurt," Kim said, revealing the most vulnerable side to her.

Desmond kissed her passionately while taking his time unbuttoning her top. "Then don't think about that…We ain't 'een gon' put it out in the universe."

Kimberlyn bit her bottom lip as she watched Desmond work. She could no longer front like she didn't want him.

"I got'chu. You hear me?"

Nodding her head, Kimberlyn savored his fervent kisses on her neck. Taking his time, he created a trail that led down her body. Desmond was ever so sensual, making sure to pay attention to every special area. However, the minute he reached her abdomen, he froze in place at the faint C-section scar on her tummy.

Desmond had no knowledge of Kimberlyn bearing a child until then. Accepting every flaw about her, he gently kissed the scar before moving lower.

After sliding her leather shorts and panties down her legs, Desmond buried his nose in her wetness. "You smell just as sweet as I remember," he whispered.

Licking her lips, Kimberlyn ran her stiletto nails over his brush waves. It'd been nearly a year since she'd experienced a man's touch, and the anticipation was driving her wild.

Desmond slowly ran his tongue over her swollen clit, before suckling it with expertise. "Taste just as sweet too..."

Kim was so sensitive to the pleasure that she tried inching away. Yet Desmond quickly grabbed her tiny waist and held her in place. “Nah. None of that,” he whispered in a hoarse tone.

“Shit, Desmond. I’ma cum,” Kim whimpered, bucking her hips against his face.

Desmond slid his middle finger inside her warm slot to prime her for his entrance. He was immediately surprised at how tight she was. “Damn, girl,” he groaned. His dick was so hard that it strained against his designer jeans.

Curling his finger upward, he tickled her spot until her juices drenched his entire hand. It didn’t take long for Kimberlyn to reach her peak. After conjuring her first orgasm, Desmond sat upright and pulled off his tee.

The sight of Desmond’s rock hard torso instantly made Kim’s pussy wetter. Staring up at him, she ran her fingertips along his six-pack. Desmond had always been incredibly fit, and the added muscle since their last encounter was certainly a turn on.

“I’m serious, Desmond,” Kim began. “Don’t start some shit, you don’t plan on finishing.”

Tired of her doubting his intentions, Desmond roughly flipped her over onto her stomach. *I guess I’ll show her ass better than I can tell her*. Coming up out his jeans and boxers, he slid inside her drenches from behind.

"*Ooooh*, shit!" Kim bellowed. She'd actually forgotten how impressive his girth was.

Kim wasn't expecting the pain that came soon after. But just as quickly it turned to pleasure.

Interlocking their fingers, Desmond created a slow rhythm. As much as he wanted to beat it up, he needed Kimberlyn to feel his passion. She was so tight that her pussy muscles snatched him back in with every thrust. "Fuck, this shit grippin'," he moaned.

"Damn, I'm about to cum again!" Kim bellowed, gripping the nearby sheets.

A nigga ain't trying to bust but this shit too good, Desmond thought. Feeling himself on the brink of exploding, he gently bit down on her neck. That automatically drove Kimberlyn crazy. Within seconds she exploded in ecstasy, her body quaking with uncontrollable orgasms. Shortly after, Desmond snatched his pole free before busting on her round ass.

"*Mmm*," he groaned, stroking it until there was nothing left. "Shit."

Once Desmond was fully depleted, he collapsed beside Kim—who was already on her way to sleep. Before closing his eyes, he placed a delicate kiss on her temple. Whatever nigga she thought she was walking down the aisle with was in for a rude awakening.

8

The following morning, Ava let herself into Desmond's home. Even though they didn't live with each other, she owned a key to his crib and usually dropped by everyday around the same time.

Dressed in a pair of drawstring black harem pants and a gray t-shirt, she looked rather casual that day. Then again, she always did when it came time to nurse her crops. After closing the large wooden double doors, Ava tossed her bag on a nearby accent table.

Just as she was making her way to the hydroponic room, Desmond appeared wearing nothing but a pair of Hanes boxers.

Pulling the wireless ear buds out her ears, Ava tried her best not to stare too hard. Truth be told, she'd always had a thing for Desmond, but was too afraid to speak on it. He treated her like a big brother, and was more loyal than any friend she'd ever known. And though Ava didn't want to mess up the good relationship they already had, she couldn't deny her attraction.

"How're my babies doing?" Ava asked, walking past him.

She was just about to put on a surgical mask to tend to her plants when Kim emerged from the hallway.

Both women were equally surprised to see the other.

"I was just finna tell you I had company," Desmond said, feeling the awkwardness in the air. Even to this day, he had no idea of Ava's feelings towards him. And if he did, it certainly wouldn't have changed the way he felt about Kimberlyn.

"Oh," was all Ava could manage to say. "In that case, I'll just come back later."

"I mean you ain't got to," Desmond quickly said.

"No, it's cool. I don't mind," Ava told him. She then looked over and gave Kim the fakest smile in the world. Deep down inside, she envied the woman parading around Desmond's home in his oversized tee.

He's never gonna learn, Ava told herself. *These bitches only want him for what he's worth. If he was with me he wouldn't have those kinds of problems.*

Grabbing her bag, Ava headed back to the front door and opened it. She was just about to walk out when she noticed a shiny black Bentley pulling into the driveway.

"Looks like you've got more company," Ava tossed over her shoulder.

Desmond quickly made his way to the front door and looked out. He hadn't even had a chance to shower and eat breakfast before the foolery popped off. Had it not been for the fact that he was sober, Desmond would've thought he was seeing shit.

"The fuck? You gotta be kiddin' me."

Easing into his circular driveway was none other than his ratchet ass baby mama, Dana. There was also a second silhouette in the passenger's seat, and he assumed it was her obnoxious girlfriend, Monica.

Dana and Monica were two peas in a pod, and one didn't move without the other. There'd even been times when Desmond accused the two of sleeping together.

"Um…is there an issue?" Kim asked behind him. She'd agreed to cooking breakfast for him, but with the way things were going she doubted that would happen. Apparently, there was a lot going on.

Desmond barely heard Kimberlyn as he stared daggers at the luxury vehicle. "What the hell is she doin' all the way out here?" he mumbled.

Killing the engine, Desmond's baby mama hopped out looking meaner than a Catholic school teacher. Even though she was nutty, Dana was a gorgeous woman with honey brown skin and green eyes. Her chestnut-colored hair was always cut in a stylish asymmetrical bob, and people rarely if ever saw her without makeup.

To be so cute, Dana was also one of the shallowest women Desmond had ever known. Even when he was faithful, she accused him of cheating. And every chick he came in contact with, he was fucking in Dana's mind. His baby mama was just too much for TV.

In all honesty, the only thing she had going for herself was good pussy—and even that had run its course over a period of time. Dana was just too fucking crazy, and Desmond no longer had the patience to tolerate it.

"What'chu doin' here?" he asked, standing in the doorway of his home.

Ava didn't bother sticking around to see the drama unfold. Instead, she hopped in her white Mercedes Benz truck and pulled off.

Monica quickly climbed out the car and headed towards his home as if she had a personal invite. She lived for drama, so Desmond couldn't say he was too surprised to see her.

"Now is that anyway to greet the mother of your child?" Dana asked with a sly smile.

9

“What’chu got goin’ on in there?” Monica asked, peeking over Desmond’s shoulder. She always was the nosey type, and she never missed an opportunity to oust him. “Why you actin’ like we can’t come in?”

“I know why. ‘Cuz he gotta bitch in there!” Dana yelled, pushing her way past him.

“Dana, man! Chill!” Desmond told her. But it was too late. As soon as she barged inside his home and took one look at Kimberlyn, she flipped.

“Mothafucka, is this why you left me and ya daughter on the west coast?! So you could live it up with some average ass bitch!”

“*Average*?! Never that, boo,” Kimberlyn said, defending herself.

“Oh, no, sweetie. Side chicks don’t even get the privilege to open they mouths in my presence. I thought you trained these hoes better than that, Dez.”

“Bitch, keep talkin’ that shit, I’ma show you just how a side chick get down!”

Open to the challenge, Dana handed her friend her purse before stepping in Kim’s face. She relished putting Desmond’s hoes in their place, and this one would be no different.

"Don't hurt her, D," Monica instigated.

"Nah. Ain't finna be none of that shit up in here," Desmond said, stepping between both women. Dana had effortlessly run off the few chicks he'd dated, but Kim was far from being easily intimidated.

Secretly, Desmond admired the way Kimberlyn held her ground against crazy ass Dana; but there was no way he was going to have his baby mama fighting.

"Then you better let yo' bitches know!" Dana snapped waving a long diamond encrusted fingernail. "These hoes need to learn where they stand. Flat out!"

Kimberlyn scoffed, clearly amused by Dana's ghetto antics. Suddenly, everything felt like déjà vu; but instead of defending her relationship with Cool, she was defending herself from another chick's man. Like Desmond had mentioned last night, she too didn't need the unnecessary drama in her life.

"Bitch, you were nonexistent a few hours ago," Kim retorted. "Take that shit up with your nigga. Not with me." She then turned to walk away, but was unexpectedly snatched by her hair from behind.

Apparently, Dana didn't take too kind to her talking recklessly. Down to get buck, Monica prepared to jump in as well, but Desmond quickly stopped her.

Whirling around, Kimberlyn threw an uncoordinated punch that luckily landed on Dana's cheek. Unfortunately, the jab wasn't strong enough to drop her—or make her release Kim's hair. Keeping a firm grip on her long locks, Dana delivered an uppercut that split Kimberlyn's bottom lip.

Before his baby mama could do any more damage, Desmond grabbed Kim up from behind. In mid-lift she kicked Dana in the rib, sending her falling against the nearby accent table. A $3400 antique Chinese vase toppled over and shattered upon impact.

The very thing Desmond had escaped was now in his face. It was all a total nightmare. He didn't need the drama then and he definitely didn't need it now.

"AYE! Calm da fuck down, Dana!" Desmond barked, grabbing his baby mama up by her throat. Manhandling her ass like only he could, he slammed her against the nearby wall.

Kimberlyn tried to swing at Dana again, but was blocked by Desmond's body standing in the way. "This bitch just put her fucking hands on me!" she screamed, blood leaking from her mouth.

"Kim, fall back."

"Lemme catch yo' ass with my nigga again, I'ma do a whole lot more!" Dana threatened. Her voice was hoarse with rage as she threatened her competition. She never got tired of eliminating them.

Desmond tried his best to keep both women from tearing each other apart. Though he had warned Kimberlyn about his crazy ex, she definitely didn't see all this coming—especially after he claimed they were officially done.

After realizing how ratchet and classless she looked, Kim finally backed off. "You know what? I don't need this shit. You ain't my nigga and I got my own headache to deal with."

"Bye, bitch! Be gone!" Dana yelled over Desmond's shoulder. She was still hemmed up against the wall as she talked shit. "And don't ever bring yo' bum ass back!"

Snatching up her purse and shoes, Kimberlyn headed to the front door in rage. Mean-mugging Monica, she dared the bitch to try to run up on her again. Fortunately, she was wise enough not to.

Kimberlyn was through with Desmond's lying ass. *A nigga will say whatever to get some pussy*, she thought. *I am so straight on him. He can have that ratchet shit*.

"Kim, hol' up right quick. I wanna talk to you," Desmond said after her.

Ignoring him, Kimberlyn slammed the front door behind her. She didn't want to hear a damn thing he had to say. Walking briskly to her parked truck, she hopped inside. The tears forming in her eyes blurred her vision, but she wouldn't dare allow them to drop over spilled milk.

"Fuck that bitch and fuck him," she said, pulling off.

10

"Good morning, sleepy head," a high-pitched voice sang. "You awake yet?"

Romeo slowly opened his eyes and looked up at a slightly familiar face. He could recall where he'd met her before he could her actual name, but that's usually how it went with him. Every morning was a different face. Most women were lucky if they even got a call the next day.

"Shit," Romeo groaned, reaching for his throbbing head. The mild hangover was a temporary consequence of late night partying but he was used to that too.

Once he dropped off Shayla, Romeo visited a couple after hour spots—where he'd met the lucky girl that was now in his bed. After a few drinks and conversation, one thing eventually led to the other.

"Don't you got somewhere to be?" Romeo asked, climbing out the king-sized bed.

"*Ugh.* Somebody's grouchy in the mornings," she teased.

Romeo took one look at the female and became annoyed all over again. He usually didn't let women sleep over because they ended up getting to comfortable like the one before him.

Helping herself, the brown-skinned cutie picked his Rolex up off the nightstand and examined it. The piece of jewelry was worth more than her house and car combined. "And not really. I was actually hoping we could get some breakfast," she smiled.

"My pops taught me as a kid that hope was for the weak," Romeo said cynically. Born to a pimp and a prostitute, his upbringing had been pretty tough, and it showed in his treatment towards women. Like father, like son. "Show yourself out. And lock the front door behind you."

Sucking her teeth, she watched as he headed inside the master bathroom. "Fucking asshole," she muttered after he closed the door.

Disappointed and offended, Romeo's one-night stand hopped out the bed and quickly dressed. He'd seemed like such a gentleman last night only to treat her like shit the following morning. "What the hell is his problem?"

After dressing hastily, she quickly walked out the bedroom. Romeo didn't reemerge from the bathroom until he finally heard the front door close behind her. *Good fucking riddance*.

Twenty minutes after his guest's departure, Romeo walked out his bedroom fully dressed and ready for the day. He was surprised when he found Ava in the kitchen munching on celery sticks while listening to Jhene Aiko. A few of his homies were also posted, lounging around as if they didn't have homes of their own. Romeo didn't mind, however. He was used to the shit. The small organization was comprised of more than just co-workers and friends. They were family.

Romeo made a quick mental note to himself to hire a personal chef. They'd had one back home, but he hadn't had a chance to get a new one since their relocation.

"What'chu doin' here? Usually, you be at Dez's by this time," Romeo said to Ava. "And why you lookin' all depressed and shit? Is it that time of month?"

A few of the niggas snickered at his question.

Romeo and Ava lived together in a 7-bedroom, 10-bathroom European estate nestled in the heart of Atlanta. Since the two of them had always been the closest from day one, they decided to split the mortgage as roommates. At only twenty-one, Ava was like the baby sister Romeo never had, and he wouldn't hesitate to hurt a motherfucker about his.

"Desmond had one of his groupies over so I told him I'd come back later," she said nonchalantly.

"Why'd you care?" Romeo asked her. Had it been him, he would've never allowed a bitch to hold up his progress—let alone his money.

"I don't," Ava quickly lied. Even though, Romeo was like a second brother to her, she'd had yet to tell him she was secretly in love with Desmond. With the way he ran through chicks, she figured he'd never be able to understand. Hell, she barely did herself.

"Aight then. Whatever, you say, V." Dropping the subject, Romeo pulled out his iPhone and scrolled through his contacts log. That day he did wake up with someone on his mind, and it certainly wasn't the bitch that had left his crib moments earlier.

***

If you a lame, nigga you ain't making no noise…

Get faded, turn up with the big boys…

Live fast, die young that's my choice…

Get money, get money like an invoice…

Groaning slightly, Shayla stirred awake after hearing her phone ring. Assuming it was her job hitting her up for a no call, no show, she anxiously grabbed her iPhone and answered. "Hello?"

"Damn, you still sleep?" Romeo asked. "Get'cha ass up, girl. A wise man once told me

'Lose an hour in the morning, and you'll be all day hunting for it'."

Shayla quickly settled down after realizing she was off work that day. Sitting up in bed, she wiped the sleep out the corners of her eyes and looked over at the digital clock. It read 11:15 a.m. Usually, she never slept that late in the day, but then again she never drank either.

"Good morning to you too," Shayla said in a muffled tone.

"Get dressed. I wanna take you out."

***

"I don't give a fuck what'chu gotta do…what strings you gotta pull…or whoever the fuck you gotta walk over to get it done, just get me up out dis bitch," Cool said.

Seated across from him was a mousy but smooth-talking defense lawyer—who was supposedly one of the best in the city. Seth Adelstein had been on Cool's case since the day the charges were slapped on him. Hell, even before then he kept Seth close like a nigga kept a side chick. In his profession, shit was bound to go south at any given moment. Keeping a lawyer on his payroll was supposed to keep his ass free. But a no-nonsense judge and strict jury changed all that shit.

Seth crossed his legs and interlocked his fingers around his knee. His cognac-colored Forzieri dress shoes looked as if they'd been spit shined. "I told you before, Christopher. You gotta meet me halfway if you want me to start performing magic tricks. An appeal certainly has to be worth the time and effort. And you hold something vital—something the FBI could really use. And as they say 'even swap no swindle."

Cool gave Seth the side eye. "You tellin' me to break the silence?" he asked, somewhat offended. Since a kid, he'd firmly believed in the no-snitch policy.

"I'm not *telling* you to do anything, Mr. Williams," Seth said. "I'm simply *implying* that if you want me to scratch your back, you have to scratch mine."

Cool sighed dejectedly before running a hand over his stubble. For the last year all he'd been concerned with was getting back on. But after Kim walked out on him yesterday, all that suddenly mattered was freedom. Besides, if his girl really was done with him he'd no longer have any residual income. Almost every niggas in his camp had turned their backs after his imprisonment, but that was to be expected in the game. Aside from Kim, no one else visited him or called in to put money on his books. His parents were dead, and Kim and Jordan were the only ones he had in his corner.

"I ain't tryin' to die in this bitch alone," he told Seth. Suddenly, loyalty and street codes were the furthest things on his mind. Cool abandoned all dignity when he leaned forward and muttered, "Fuck it. For my freedom, I'll sing like a mufuckin' canary."

11

"Did you see how that nigga was protecting that bitch?! Girl, I could cut that motherfucker for disrespecting me!" Dana screamed. "Talkin' 'bout he moved here for opportunities. Looked like he moved to parlay with a bunch of bitches!"

She, Monica, and her 8-year old daughter Destiny were inside a suite at the St. Regis Hotel. Until she figured things out with her baby daddy, it was Dana and Destiny's temporary residence.

Dana had already made her mind up. Either she was going back to Cali with Desmond, or he was putting her in a crib in the A. Either way she planned on being a thorn in his side. Monica was just along for the ride since she loved entertainment.

"Mommy, am I gonna be able to see daddy?" Destiny asked in a small voice. Although she knew her mother was in a bad mood, she couldn't hide her excitement of rekindling with her father.

Whenever Desmond wanted to break things off with Dana she purposely kept his daughter away to annoy him. She figured their child was more than enough leverage to make him stay. Sadly, she was wrong.

Desmond didn't even know that she'd used a similar tactic to trap him with a baby. Poking holes in their condoms finally paid off after several attempts…and nine months later Destiny was born.

No matter how hard Desmond thought he could shake Dana, it would never happen. They were bonded by a child, and he had no choice but to put up with her for life. And she definitely planned on making it a living hell if she couldn't be a part of it.

"Girl, get out my fucking mouth and watch cartoons!" Dana snapped. Her mothering skills were lacking since she spent most of her time chasing after Desmond. Now, seven years later, it still never got tiring.

Afraid of being chastised, Destiny quickly focused on *SpongeBob*. She, like everyone else, knew how crazy her mama was.

"Girl, I can't believe any of that shit," Monica instigated. "If it was me, I'd be slashing a motherfucker's tires out." She loved to boast what she'd do in similar situations, but she hadn't had a man since '06. Instead of building her own relationship, she settled for a front row seat to Dana and Desmond's.

Grabbing her cellphone, Dana called her baby daddy for the seventh time that afternoon. As expected, he didn't even bother answering. Had he known his daughter was with her he would have, but Dana was keeping that bit of info to herself.

When it was clear Desmond wouldn't pick up, Dana sent a tasteless text message she knew would him rattle him up. *I'm only just getting started mothafucka. Get rid of these hoes or I will. Now play wit it.*

***

"About damn time!" Rita hounded Kim the minute she walked inside her home. She'd been babysitting Jordan all night even though Kim told her she'd only be out a few hours. "Where the hell you been, girl? I told you I had—Oh, my God! What is that on your shirt? Is that blood?"

Rita was Kimberlyn's forty-seven year old live-in aunt who occasionally helped out with Jordan. She had also raised Kim since the age of twelve after losing her mother in an automobile accident. The unexpected death of her sister took a heavy toll on Rita, and eventually she turned to drugs and alcohol to numb the pain. Over time, it went from her caring for Kim to Kim caring for her.

Though Rita had thankfully kicked the habits, her finances had taken a major hit. Four years ago, she lost her home and Cool graciously stepped up by moving her in. After all, it wasn't like they didn't have the room in their four-bedroom Craftsman home.

Back when Cool was the man, he'd brought Kimberlyn the 4100 sq. ft. house and paid for it in cash. He had also hired an interior decorator to spruce up the place to his fiancé's liking. Kimberlyn felt like a queen…But soon after she discovered the side chicks he'd also brought homes for behind her back.

Rita never did bother with getting back on her feet. Cool had her and Kimberlyn spoiled senselessly, and instead of seeking independence, she became a permanent addition to the household family.

"It's nothing Auntie Rita," Kim said, waving her off. "Look, I had a long night."

"Well, I could have *too* had you returned on time! Yo' ass too damn old to be out in the streets fightin' like you ain't gotta child at home." Rita huffed. She was a spitting image of Kimberlyn's mother, and even had the sass to go with it. "By the way, Cool called this morning. He was saying something about his case being overturned," she explained. "I told him you were out with Shayla. He wasn't too happy about not being able to talk to you."

Kimberlyn grimaced at the mention of her baby's father. He was the last person she wanted to hear about or speak to—especially after all the drama with Desmond.

"That nigga ain't gettin' out no time soon," Kim waved her off. "And right now Cool is really the *least* of my worries."

12

The following morning, Romeo and his camp had the entire mansion foggy with thick marijuana clouds. With every fresh batch, they tested the goods personally to make sure they were ready for distribution.

Ab-Soul's "*Terrorist Threats*" poured through the built in speakers. It was only 10 a.m., but they had the place turnt up. Thankfully, their home was tucked off in the cut away from nosey neighbors with a good sense of smell.

Romeo blew several large O's before blowing a smaller one through all of them. He'd been smoking herb since the age of twelve and knew damn near every trick in the book. "Aye, I think I wanna buy a strip club," he said, eyes bloodshot red.

Ava coughed several times before struggling to respond. When she realized she couldn't, she burst out laughing at her own master concoction..

"It's settled then," Romeo said after no one spoke up.

A few of his homies laughed and told him how much of a clown he was. But on the low he had it all mapped out. A new club could serve as a front; after all, where was the number one spot most celebrities liked to frequent?

“I ain’t fuckin’ wit’ ya’ll today,” Romeo laughed, standing to his feet.

“Where you goin’?” Ava whined.

“Finna get up with a new friend,” Romeo said over his shoulder. Once he was alone in the hallway, he pulled out his phone and hit up Shayla.

Surprisingly, she answered on the second ring. “Hey.”

“Mornin’. I see yo’ ass up and at ‘em today, huh?”

Shayla laughed. “I, um, took your advice,” she told him.

“Right, right,” he chuckled. “Shit, you hungry? Let’s get somethin’ to eat at Peachtree on Watershed. I read somewhere they had the best brunch in the A.”

“Read?” Shayla repeated subconsciously.

Romeo chuckled at the surprise in her voice. “Yeah…A nigga read sometimes,” he told her.

“I wasn’t saying it like that,” Shayla lied.

“Yeah, I hear you. But look, you gon’ meet me in an hour or what?” Romeo was tired of her stalling. His assertiveness was something Shayla wasn’t used to, but she couldn’t deny that it was a turn on. In his world, he was used to making demands, and in hers she was used to following them.

"It may take me longer. I don't have a car," Shayla admitted.

"What? Time out. What'chu mean you ain't got no car?"

Shayla laughed nervously, not expecting his bold reaction. "I…I don't have a car," she repeated timidly. Shayla didn't know why Romeo was making such a big deal about it. She knew plenty of people who didn't own a set of wheels.

Romeo sighed into the receiver dramatically. "Man, change of plans. I'll be to you in about an hour. You better be ready too," he told her. "And not just for a date…For a nigga like me."

Before Shayla could ask what he meant, Romeo disconnected the call.

"Oh my God," she smiled to herself. "What did I just get myself into?"

Snatching the covers off her body, Shayla quickly hopped out the bed and ran to the bathroom to shower. Something told her, Romeo was going to give her a run for her money.

***

Shayla's eyebrows furrowed in confusion as she and Romeo pulled into Mercedes-Benz of Buckhead. Earlier they had agreed to lunch at *Watershed on Peachtree* so she didn't know why they were pulling into a car dealership instead.

Romeo didn't bother elaborating as he parked and turned off the vehicle. That day he was driving a black on black Bentley Coupe with peanut butter guts. It was quite obvious to Shayla that he liked fast things. Too bad she wasn't. Shayla could only hope she didn't bore him after a while. They seemed like total opposites, and she was sure he noticed it too.

I wonder what he sees in me, Shayla thought. *If he sees anything at all…*

Don't be ridiculous. He wouldn't be kicking it with you right now if he didn't see anything, her conscience argued.

Together, they climbed out the car and headed towards the building. Shayla was surprised when Romeo took her hand in his and led the way. A part of her missed that subtle physical contact with a man. However, the other half questioned his motives.

Shayla thought about her recent breakup with Dexter, and wondered if she was truly ready for something real. Before she could figure it out an anxious salesman walked up to them and asked if he could be of any assistance.

Romeo pulled off his $450 Gucci sunglasses and folded them close. "I'm tryna see what dem pre-owned cars hittin' on."

"Certainly!" he said giddily. "My name is Bob by the way. Do you have any specific features you're looking for?"

As the two men talked business, Shayla's mind wandered to Kimberlyn and how her night ended with ol' boy. *That bitch ain't even call me to see if I made it home okay. She's gonna hear about that shit too*, Shayla told herself.

"Right here we have the 2014 Mercedes-Benz C250. It's an automatic 7-speed and only has 9,000 miles on it."

Romeo turned to Shayla for her opinion. "How you feel about this?" he asked.

Looking the four-door sedan over, Shayla nodded her head in approval. "I like it...But you took me as someone who liked faster cars."

Romeo and the salesman laughed in unison.

"I ain't da one that's gon' be driving it." Pointing to Shayla, he said. "You are."

Shayla's mouth dropped open in shock. "Wait—what? You're trying to buy this for—no, no. Romeo, I can't let you do that." She then turned to the salesman. "It's a no go—"

“Shayla…,” Romeo interrupted. Placed his hands on her small shoulders, he tried his best to calm her. Her humility was so adorable. “Look, I love where ya head and heart’s at…but learn to accept when a real nigga wanna do somethin’ nice for you.”

Shayla opened her mouth to respond but closed it after realizing she didn’t have anything to say. No man had ever gone the extra mile for her—not even Dex.

Taking her silence for acceptance, Romeo turned to face the awaiting salesman. “We’ll take it.”

13

A few men turned their heads to admire Shayla as she headed towards the bar. Every Saturday afternoon she met up with Kimberlyn for wings and hookah at *Cloud 9.* It was a weekly ritual the girls had been doing for nearly three years.

With all the "male drama" in their lives, it was vital they get together once in a while to dish their dirt. Shayla looked beautiful that day in a denim pencil skirt, white crop top, and studded open toe white booties. Her ass sat up nicely in her attire, commanding attention from every fella in the room. For once, there was in confidence Shayla's stride—and it had a lot to do with the mysterious Romeo.

"Bitch, I know I ain't just see you pull up in the foreign though," Kimberlyn greeted. Unlike Shayla, she was a dressed a bit more casually in jeans and a black sleeveless turtleneck. Her long hair was pulled high in a ponytail, and she wore minimal makeup. That definitely wasn't like Kim, but the niggas had her all out her element.

Shayla slid into the empty barstool beside her friend and flagged down the bartender. "Girl, yes. I've had quite the morning—"

"Wait, before you tell me, why did I just find out Cool might be getting an early release?"

Shayla gasped in shock after hearing the news. His sentence had been firm the day of the trial, so she couldn't imagine what brought about the change. Usually, guys who faced Cool's charges weren't anywhere near as lucky to see an appeal.

"What are you gonna do if he gets out early?" Shayla asked.

"What the hell you think? I'ma keep living," Kimberlyn said matter-of-factly.

"I mean are you *done* with him…or…"

"I'm over that life, Shay. And at the end of the day he has no choice but to respect it," Kimberlyn said. "That chapter in my life is done. I'm through with exposing my son to that shit. And I'm through with being a part of it."

At that moment, the bartender rushed over and inquired about their beverages. And it was just in time too, considering the tension. Only Cool could get Kimberlyn so worked up.

Shayla went ahead and ordered her usual, Peach vodka, and Kimberlyn an Apple martini. Once their first round arrived, Kim went on to explain her long night and early morning with Desmond. She also spared no details when it came to the run-in with his baby mama.

"What is up with you and these low lives you attract?" Shayla asked, shaking her head. Kimberlyn sure could pick them.

"That's just the thing," Kimberlyn said. "I never remembered Desmond being that type. When we first met, he was upfront about her—about everything...I'm not proud of it, but I made the decision to roll with the punches anyway. I don't see why he would lie about the shit now."

"Seasons change and so do people," Shayla reminded her.

"True," Kim agreed. "But Desmond wasn't like that. From Cool I could expect it…but Dez…He isn't anything like Cool." There was a faraway look in Kimberlyn's eyes as she reflected on the passionate night they shared. She longed for many more, but it was obvious Dana wasn't having it. And Kim had never been one to willingly share.

Shayla snorted, interrupting her thoughts. "That I *could* believe. Cool is irredeemable filth," she said. "I would hope it couldn't get much worse than that."

Kimberlyn was just about to respond before she saw a familiar face walk in the lounge. "Oh, shit. Don't look now."

Doing the exact opposite, Shayla turned in her seat and literally froze at the sight of him. Headed straight their way was none other than her ex-boyfriend, Dexter. Even with everything they'd been through Shayla couldn't deny how attractive he looked. A few months felt like forever since the last time she'd seen him.

Dressed in a $325 Maison Kitsuné hoodie, black jeans, and classic black Timberland boots, Dexter always had been the trendy type. His lineup was crisp and his deep chocolate skin had a natural glow. Dexter was fine as all hell…but he was also a liar and a cheater—and Shayla would never forget that.

"Damn, we gotta change up our habits," she told Kim. Her ex was the last person she expected to pop in on her.

Dexter's Clive Christian cologne reached them well before he did. "What's up, Kimmy?" he greeted. Shoving his hands in his pockets, he looked over at Shayla. "Can I talk to you for a second, Shay?"

There was an awkward period of silence amongst the three of them before Shayla finally responded. "I'm politicking with my girl," she said, hoping he'd take the hint.

Dexter looked over at Kimberlyn and asked, "Do you mind?"

Holding her hands up in mock surrender, she said, "Not at all. Do you."

If Shayla were the violent type, she would've slapped the shit out of Kimberlyn. *I shouldn't even be entertaining him at this very moment*, she told herself. *But I guess the least I can do is hear him out. Besides, it's not like I didn't ignore his phone calls for the last couple months.*

"Fine," Shayla said, climbing out her seat.

Together they walked out the front door so they could talk in privacy, without the background music. Once they were alone, in the comforts of themselves, Dexter began. "First, I wanna tell you I miss the hell outta you, Shay. You lookin' real good today too, I see you."

Unimpressed, Shayla folded her arms and tried to pretend his words didn't affect her.

"To be honest, a nigga been sittin' out here the last thirty minutes waitin' for you to come. I know you and ya girl frequent this place like clockwork," he said. "Anyway, I saw you pull up in ya new whip. I started to go in after you right away, but had to get my choice of words together."

Shayla remained silent as she listened. This was their first time talking civilly since their breakup, and it felt strange. His act of betrayal was one that couldn't be forgiven or forgotten easily.

"So…when you get da new ride?" Dexter asked, looking over at her shiny Mercedes. Truthfully, he just wanted to take the focus off himself.

Romeo had gotten the car washed and waxed before they pulled off the lot. The tires even gleamed with polish. It'd been nearly eight years since Shayla had her very own car, and Romeo put her in one without batting an eyelash. They barely knew each other, and he'd already done something for her no man had ever.

"Ironically today," Shayla finally spoke up. "And I didn't buy it. A friend did." She refused to take credit for Romeo's blessing—especially if it made Dexter jealous.

The look of envy in his eyes immediately let her know he was. "*A friend*?" Dexter repeated skeptically. "We only been apart a few months and you already got niggas buyin' you cars? Hell, if I ain't know any better I'd say dat *friend* been around, if you catch my drift."

Shayla instantly propped her hands on her curvy hips. "Are you insinuating that I cheated on you while we were together?" She was morbidly offended considering the actual circumstances. Shayla was as loyal as they came, and Dexter knew it.

"Aye, if the shoe fits," he retorted.

Tossing her hands in the air, Shayla prepared to walk off. "You know what? I don't have time for this."

Suddenly, Dexter latched onto her forearm. "Hold up. Damn, I ain't mean all dat. Shit, what you expect from me, Shay? I been missin' you like crazy. A mufucka barely can sleep at night, and come to find out you already got suitors…Mufuckas puttin' you in cars and shit. Somethin' I ain't ever been able to do. How the hell you think that's supposed to make me feel as a man?"

"I honestly don't care," Shayla told him. "This conversation is over. Now let go of my arm. You're hurting me."

Instead of granting her wish, Dexter's grip tightened. Apart from being a cheater, he was also known to have a temper. Although he had never gotten overly violent with Shayla, he did have a tendency to get a bit rough when he didn't get his way. Raised with a silver spoon in his mouth, Dexter despised being told no.

"Come on now. Why you actin' like this, Shay? All I wanna do is talk. Damn, why you givin' me hell?"

"Did you hear me? I said let go of me."

"Is there a problem?" Kimberlyn asked, stepping outside. There was a genuine look of concern on her face as she waited for a response. If in fact some shit were to pop off, she had no problem going in her purse. Kim definitely didn't play when it came to her girls.

Dexter finally released Shayla's arm, leaving a nasty purple handprint behind. "Aight then. I'ma get up wit'chu later. 'Cuz this ain't over, Shay," he said, walking to his parked BMW. "You got da right one. Believe dat. I ain't ever finna sit back and let a nigga take what's mine."

In silence, Shayla and Kimberlyn watched him pull off, burning rubber in the process. Something told her that wasn't going to be their last run in.

14

It was ten minutes to six when Desmond and Romeo arrived at their newly purchased warehouse in Old Fourth Ward district. The two obtained the building merely to store large quantities of marijuana coming in from Cali by the metric ton.

As a front, they also bought out a truck company to transport product straight from L.A. Keeping suspicions down was the name of the game, and Romeo and Desmond played it with full expertise.

Prior to moving down, they'd purchased the property and were finally taking the time out for a walkthrough.

The old industrial building reeked of old age, but it had an awesome structure and expansive space. With a little tender, loving, care the place would be ship-shape for proper usage in no time.

"How you feel about it?" Desmond asked, walking around the main area. Once things got a bit more organized he planned on bringing in more workers to manufacture three times as much product. Ava was against the idea of course, not wanting to reveal her tactics to strangers; but Desmond was sure with a little persuading she'd eventually give in. Growing out of his house was getting old; they were in the big leagues now.

Besides, more product meant more revenue, and Ava ultimately couldn't argue with that.

"Shit, I'm fuckin' with it," Romeo answered half-heartedly. Truth be told, his mind was on Shayla. For some strange reason, he couldn't get her out his head—which was out of the norm for a nigga like him.

"So I seen you creep off with ole girl from da club last night," Desmond said, changing the subject. "Were you able to redeem yaself?"

Romeo chuckled and ran a hand over his fresh cut. "Nah, homie. We ain't 'een go there last night," he told him. "But I did make up for it dis mornin'. Took her to da dealership and put her in somethin' nice."

"Wait a second, bruh. Da chick you met *last night*? Da one you just said you ain't go there with." Desmond burst out laughing hysterically. "Oh, shit. So you buyin' bitches cars now, huh? Dat's what's hot in da streets, my nigga?" he teased.

Romeo joined him in laughter. His antics amused even him sometimes. "Aye, fuck you. I get it back, fool. Easy."

Shaking his head in disbelief, Desmond could only admire his friend's injudicious attitude. Romeo didn't flinch when it came to spending money on hoes. He'd even sent one chick through law school. Desmond only hoped Shayla was worth his paper and time. "Fool, you always was a trick ass nigga," he laughed. "Anyway, tell me why my baby moms came up to da crib wildin'?"

Romeo's eyes shot open in shock. "*Bruh…*?!"

"Dawg, I had to pull da bitch off Kim."

Romeo couldn't stop himself from laughing at his boy's misfortune. "See, homie. I done told ya ass 'bout wifin' these hood hoes. Da pussy ain't worth da headache."

"Shit, tell me about it," Desmond agreed. Romeo was all too familiar with Dana's antics. And now that she was here in Atlanta, things were only about to get worse.

***

Parked across the street from the warehouse in her rental was Dana. Desmond had no idea she'd been clocking his every move since her arrival.

Dana wouldn't hesitate to blackmail his ass if need be. At the end of the day, she knew too much about him and his operation to go down without a fight.

"This nigga can play with me if he want to," Dana said. "I will fuck up his whole shit."

***

Later on that evening, Romeo and Shayla met up for dinner at *The Capital Grille* in

Buckhead. Normally, he didn't like entertaining chicks that didn't put out on the first night—but Shayla was different. Being around her felt like a breath of fresh air, and though she was unlike what he was used to, Romeo welcomed the challenge.

As they were seated at their table, Shayla tried her best not to notice the lustful looks from the waitress. Apparently, she wasn't the only one who found Romeo attractive.

He looked handsome and flashy in a blue camouflage Versace shirt, white jeans, and spiked blue sneakers with the bloody bottoms. Draped around his neck was a sparkling gold Mercedes chain.

Shayla was more than curious to know what he did for a living; but felt it was too early to ask. *Maybe he'll tell me when he thinks the time is right.*

Shayla damn near lost her appetite when Romeo shot the young waitress an innocent wink. *I am so not used to this type of guy*, she thought to herself. Romeo was an open flirt, and she'd always been the jealous type. *I don't know how this could ever work.*

Relax, Shayla scolded herself. *We're just on a date. It's not like the man asked me to walk down the aisle. Stop thinking about what could go wrong, and start thinking about what could go right. Besides, he's not my man.*

“Can I get you two started with some drinks? Our featured wine today is the Markham Merlot. Its bright cherry and blueberry flavors are meld with plump tannins. I can promise you, it’s very sweet to the taste,” she said, looking specifically at Romeo.

“I bet it is,” he said. “We’ll take two of those…and make one of ‘em extra light,” Romeo added, giving Shayla the side eye.

Shayla’s cheeks flushed in embarrassment. She could only imagine how foolish she must’ve looked tipsy last night.

After the waitress scribbled down their beverages and walked off, Romeo decided to make light conversation.

“So…Am I winning you over yet, Miss Shayla?”

Smiling, she looked down at her manicured hands. “I don’t know. It’s only day two...and you started off kinda rocky.”

Romeo leaned forward and interlocked his fingers. His stare was so intense that it made Shayla too nervous to keep eye contact. “You don’t know. *Really*?” he chuckled. “Come on now. Cut ya boy some slack.”

“I mean, you seem like a nice guy and all…But I can tell you’re used to a different breed,” Shayla explained. “You don’t have to try so hard with me, Romeo. And you certainly don't have to go out your way financially."

"Is that right?"

"Up until recently, I've always been pretty independent."

Romeo was shocked by her humbleness. Most females he fucked with loved the spoiled treatment whereas Shayla was too proud to accept it.

"And what changed that?" Romeo asked, suddenly peaked by her life.

Shayla hesitated for a second. "Truthfully…a breakup…"

"Damn…I'm sorry to hear that," Romeo told her. "But I kinda figured."

Shayla's perfectly arched brows rose in surprise. "How so?" she asked curiously.

"I don't know. I just notice lil' shit about you," he said. "You lowkey uptight. And you quick to snap on a nigga at da drop of a dime. It's obvious some mufucka left a bad taste in ya mouth."

"I didn't snap on you when you were eye-humping the waitress," she challenged.

Romeo scoffed and shook his head in amusement. Shayla was feistier than he imagined, but that only made shit more interesting.

"I'll take you bein' jealous as a good sign," he smiled, reaching for her hand. All of a sudden, he noticed the dark purplish bruise on her forearm and became alarmed. "How dat happen?"

Shayla quickly covered the bruise with her hand, too embarrassed to tell him the truth. "It's nothing. Really..."

There was a short period of silence between them before Romeo spoke. "Look, I know we just met each other and shit, but if I'ma fuck with you, I need you to be a hunnid wit' me," he said. "Lemme know if I gotta check a nigga."

Where Romeo was from, niggas who put their hands on women were treated like the bitches they were. And now that he was digging Shayla, he refused to let anyone hurt her.

"My ex…Dexter," she began. "We had an exchange of words, he got a little physical—but it was nothing serious."

"Dat don't look like 'nothin' serious'," Romeo said. "And it wasn't there earlier…which means ya'll got up after me and you." He couldn't hide the envy in his tone as he put two and two together.

Shayla giggled before shaking her head at Romeo. "I'll take you bein' jealous as a good sign."

That instantly eased the tension and brought a smile to his face. "Maybe. Anyway what buddy do for a livin'?" Romeo asked, somewhat interested in her ex now. Truth be told, he just wanted to see what the competition was looking like—if there was any at all.

"He's a trainer at the Planet Fitness in Chamblee Tucker," Shayla told him. "But enough about him. Just talking about my ex gives me a headache," she admitted.

"Fa'sho," Romeo agreed. "I can dig dat." Out of respect, he decided to drop the subject for now. But the issue at hand definitely wouldn't go unaddressed.

15

"So how you like it?" Romeo asked Shayla on their way out the restaurant.

"Other than the waitress flirting with you every so often, it was a pleasant experience," she retorted.

They were just about to walk outside when Romeo gently grabbed her forearm. Stopping Shayla in her tracks, he slowly backed her against a nearby wall. A few people passed them by but at that moment they only saw each other.

Romeo softly pinned his body against Shayla's before lifting her chin up towards him. Her heart fluttered uncontrollably in her tummy since he had caught her off guard. Even though it was too early for a kiss she didn't want to stop him from possibly taking one.

Damn. What is it about this dude, Shayla asked herself.

He's trouble, she thought. *But some enjoyment is worth the trouble...*

Romeo's HERMÈS cologne surrounded Shayla, leaving her intoxicated. It'd been quite some time since a man made her knees buckle…and Romeo was breaking her down by day.

Leaning downward, he moved in as if he were preparing to kiss Shayla. His warm breath smelled of the mint he'd just popped after dinner.

Shayla's common sense urged her to stop him before things moved too fast, but her body begged otherwise. Shayla didn't budge an inch when his strong arms went to her tiny waist. He had so much sex appeal that it was hard to turn him away. From his looks, to his swag, Romeo was dangerously undeniable.

"Don't worry about her…She where she need to be and you where you need to be. Feel me?"

Shayla's heart beat in anticipation as she waited for their lips to connect—but sadly it never happened. Pulling back, Romeo took her by the hand and led her out the four star restaurant. *Talk about crushing a girl's dreams. This nigga knows exactly what he's doing*, she thought to herself as he guided her to his Porsche.

Once inside, Shayla fastened her seatbelt and turned to face Romeo. "Why all that back there?" she asked curiously.

"Why what?" Romeo asked, purposely fucking with her.

"Back in the restaurant…You acted as if you wanted to kiss me."

Romeo smirked, revealing a sexy deep dimple. "You say the shit like you *want* a kiss," he teased.

Biting her bottom lip, Shayla carefully considered whether or not to utter her next choice of words. "Maybe I did," she said, finally giving in.

Romeo hit the push to start button and turned to look at Shayla. She was so damn sexy that night it should've been a sin. The bashful young woman who'd cursed him out a day ago was rapidly letting her guards down. That realization left him excited and apprehensive; excited because of the possibilities…and nervous because of the possibilities.

"How 'bout this," Romeo began. "If you wanna kiss, you gimme one…"

Shayla laughed and shook her head at his pettiness. Truth be told, she actually found it cute and amusing. "That's how you wanna play it?" she asked, giggling.

"Why not?" Romeo smiled.

PartyNextDoor's "*Recognize*" poured through the speakers as Shayla unfastened her seatbelt. Romeo didn't expect her to lean over and press her lips against the corner of his mouth. And while the peck was innocent, Romeo was impressed by her assertiveness nonetheless. From day one Shayla had played the shy role to perfection. It was refreshing to know she didn't have a problem going after something she wanted. It let Romeo know exactly where her head was at.

16

Kimberlyn was giving her a son, Jordan a bath that night when her cellphone rang. A part of her didn't want to answer for fear that it was Cool. Once in a while he got a hold of a C.O.'s phone after call hours. At the moment, she didn't feel like being bothered with him.

Maybe it's Shayla or Nina, Kim thought. However, the moment she saw the caller ID, she instantly frowned at the name displayed.

"What do you want, Desmond?" Kimberlyn answered, unenthused.

"…You…"

CLICK!

After placing her phone down, Kim continued with her task at hand. Jordan seemingly didn't have a care in the world as he allowed her to wash his hair. Like his mother, he too had a headful. He also had her green eyes, and ironically the same beauty mark. Jordan was Kimberlyn's entire world; the one thing that made life worth living for. And she was willing to do whatever to ensure he didn't end up being like Cool.

No sooner than three seconds of hanging up did her cell ring again. "What?!" she yelled into the receiver.

"Ugh, bitch. Somebody snappy," Nina laughed.

Kimberlyn sighed deeply after realizing it was her girl. She was so upset that she didn't even look at the caller ID before answering.

"Girl, you don't even know the half of it," Kim said. Before she could fill her friend in on her life's latest drama, the line began clicking. "Hold up, girl, don't hang up." Before Nina could protest, Kimberlyn clicked over. "What do you want, Dez? Your girl already made it clear she ain't sharing—"

"Aye, check this out. My baby moms don't run shit," Desmond told her. "She don't control my life and she definitely don't control who I fuck."

When Desmond came back in town Kimberlyn assumed they could pick things up where they left off, but apparently his BM had her own agenda.

"Look, I really ain't tryin' to have some bullshit wedge us apart, K," Desmond told her. In his voice was sincerity, but Kim was unsure if she could trust him. "The first time it was da distance and da circumstances," he continued. "We ain't got no obstacles other than a bitch dat miss da D. That's all that is."

"Is that *all* you have to say about the situation?" Kimberlyn asked. She'd totally forgotten about Nina being on the other end.

There was a short silence on Desmond's end as he pondered her question. "What else you want me to say, babe?"

"Um…I don't know. An apology should've definitely been in order." Had it not been for him explaining himself Kim would've hung up on him a second time.

Desmond didn't miss the sarcasm in her tone; but he was willing to let her have it if that meant squashing their differences. "My bad about all dat shit earlier. I guarantee you won't have to deal with that again."

"What makes you think I wanna deal with *you* again?" Kimberlyn countered.

Desmond didn't miss a beat. "'Cuz you still on da phone with a nigga…"

His response was simple and straightforward. Even Kimberlyn couldn't deny that she was still somewhat captivated by Desmond—especially after their rendezvous last night.

"What'chu gettin' into tonight?" he asked. Desmond figured Kim's silence was an open invite to get back in her good graces.

"Nothing much. I'ma be holdin' the house down since my aunt's out. In other words, I don't have a babysitter."

"Shit, dat's cool. You should let me slide through and chill. I could grab us somethin' to eat on da way," he said. "Maybe twist up after you put your son to sleep. Hell, I'm happy just to see you and be able to spend time wit'chu."

Kimberlyn's cheeks became warm as Desmond played on her emotions. He'd always known what to say. It was the same game that had dazzled her some five years ago. Pausing, Kimberlyn deliberated his enticing offer. Although she was really feeling Desmond, she had never brought another man inside of Cool's home.

Fuck Cool. That nigga ain't going anywhere anytime soon. Why not live a little?

"Give me an hour to put the baby to sleep. I'll text you my address." Disconnecting the call, Kimberlyn looked over at Jordan who was splashing in the water while playing with his toys.

Apprehension washed over her, but she quickly shook it off.

17

"Wow. I can't believe you live here."

Shayla tried her best not to appear awestruck as she walked through Romeo's luxurious palace. Expensive décor and breathtaking furniture offered a regal feel to his home, and secretly Shayla felt privileged for the invite. Dexter came from wealth but not even him or his family was living this good.

Shayla had to keep her jaw from hitting the polished marble floors. To say she was impressed was an understatement. Romeo was living like a king, and it instantly made her curious about him and his mysterious career. *Maybe he's a rapper. Nah. He doesn't look like the type*.

"I'm surprised the place empty," Romeo said, leading the way. "Usually, I can never get a second to myself to think in dis mufucka."

Taking her by the hand, he led her through the spacious living room. Approaching a wall of floor-to-ceiling glass windows, Romeo hit a button that automatically made them slide open. Beyond that was a vast Olympic pool with built in lighting.

The back of the house was decorated with tasteful outdoor furniture, a fire pit, and a sleek gourmet grille. Romeo's house had every essential entertainment item. *This boy lives in a freaking mansion.* Shayla's curiosity was now gnawing at her patience. She had to know what he did.

Before Shayla could question him, Romeo cut her off. "Take a dip with me?" he asked, pulling his shirt over his head.

Shayla's heart stopped beating at the sight of his rock hard torso. Every muscle was perfectly defined, and tattoos painted his body like a canvas. The pool lights reflected beautifully off his brown skin. Shayla was so turned Romeo's thug appeal and the mystery behind him.

"I…I don't have a swimsuit," she stammered, rubbing the goose bumps on her arm. It was relatively warm outside, but her nipples were erect. It was no secret Romeo had her hot and bothered.

"Neither do I," he told her, unbuttoning his jeans.

Shayla watched as he stepped out his pants. His athletic legs were a sight to behold, and she wouldn't have been surprised if he hit the gym every day.

Wearing nothing but a pair of navy briefs, Romeo climbed into the sparkling pool. Once he was halfway submerged, he grabbed his cellphone and scrolled through a few settings. Seconds later, The Weeknd's "*King of the Fall*" began playing on the wireless speakers outside.

He plays too much, Shayla thought smiling to herself. Coincidentally, she loved The Weeknd.

After setting the mood just right, Romeo reached in his jeans and pulled out rolling papers and a sack. “You smoke?” he asked, spreading the contents out. Breaking it down, he strategically placed it inside a folded paper.

Shayla eyed the pink frosted hemp and frowned. “Back in college I tried it a few times. But even then it wasn’t really my thing.”

When Romeo expertly licked the joint close, Shayla’s clit jumped with excitement.

“That’s ‘cuz you ain’t smoke dis,” he bragged. Firing up the spliff, he took a strong inhale and passed it to her.

For several seconds, Shayla simply stared at his outstretched hand unsure if she should take it or not. Normally, she wasn’t one to live on the wild side, being the prude she was. As a matter of fact, Kimberlyn was the only exciting element in her life.

What the hell? Walking over to Romeo, Shayla knelt down and took it.

“You so cute,” he told her. Romeo was amused by Shayla’s irrepressible innocence. A nigga like him would taint her good girl rep. “Aye, that shit fye, so pull it light.”

Heeding his warning, Shayla took a small inhale before releasing it through slightly parted lips. The scent was both pungent and pleasant; and it instantly left her lightheaded.

Coughing faintly, Shayla handed the joint back to Romeo.

"So what's up?" he asked. "You gon' play timid still…or you gon' come up out dem clothes?"

Normally, Shayla didn't move so fast when it came to guys—but Romeo wasn't just any guy. There was something about him that was irresistible…something that made it hard for her to say no.

Live a little, her conscience whispered.

Finally making her mind up, Shayla slowly slid out her heels and clothes. Romeo's eyes never left hers as he watched her undress seductively. Wearing nothing but a black lace bra set, Shayla tiptoed to the pool and gradually submerged herself.

And she gon give it up 'cuz she know I might like it…

And she gon give it up 'cuz she know I might like it…

The Toronto singer crooned in the distance as Shayla slowly swam over towards Romeo. His pole was already stiff by the time she reached him. Pulling her close, he leaned down and covered her mouth with his.

Shayla wrapped her arms around Romeo's neck and melted into his strong body. Chills ran down her spine as he cupped her round ass while kissing her passionately. Somewhat buzzed off the herb, Shayla's sexual senses were on high alert. Romeo was both aggressive and gentle with his touches as he gripped and held her firmly.

"I never move this fast," Shayla said breathlessly.

Romeo placed delicate kisses along her neck and collarbone as he held her close. He couldn't believe what he was about to say next, but he really was digging Shayla. "We can stop if you ain't feelin' it…"

Wrapping her chocolate legs around his waist, Shayla kissed him with the passion of a wife. She was too far gone to turn back now, and too bashful to admit the weed had her uncontrollably aroused. "I want to," Shayla whispered.

Keeping a firm hold on her, Romeo climbed out the pool and carried her inside the house. Laughing the entire time, it felt good to have fun with a guy. It had been so long that she'd forgotten the experience.

Romeo didn't bother closing the glass doors behind him as he carried her to the master bathroom. Four marble pillars surrounded a spacious jet tub overlooking the pool they were just in. Beside that was a huge, stone walk-in shower with a rainfall sprout and built in speakers.

Shayla didn't protest when he stepped inside the shower and turned on the water. Easing out of his hold, she slowly pulled off her last two articles of clothing.

Romeo kept his intense stare locked on Shayla as he slid out his soaking wet briefs.

Her eyes instantly shot open at the impressive length of his pipe. Stroking it gently in his hand, Romeo grabbed a handful of her breast and squeezed lightly. "You flex like you sweet and shit, but I know it's a naughty side to yo' ass."

Shayla closed her eyes and savored his warm touches. "Maybe…," she teased.

Romeo's large hand glided down her flat tummy before settling on the spot between her thighs.

"*Mmm.*"

Dipping his finger inside her drenches, Romeo tickled her love spot. After getting her good and primed, he wiped her juices across her swollen clit. Ever so gently, he kneaded the sensitive piece of flesh between his fingers. Romeo knew just how to touch and tease a woman. He had long mastered the art of sexual reflexology.

Shayla had to grab the shower walls just to keep her balance. "That feels so good," she whispered. Her conscience screamed for her to slow down, but her body begged for Romeo to keep going.

Trapped in a state of ecstasy, she hungrily crushed her lips against his. In all her twenty-four years, Shayla had never wanted someone so badly in her life.

"Turn dat ass around," Romeo demanded. He mannishly maneuvered her to his liking. With her plump ass tooted out just the way he wanted, Romeo positioned himself behind Shayla. "You gon' be my bitch when it's all said and done." Grabbing a fistful of her long hair, he spread her legs apart and rested his shaft against her base.

"Romeo, hold up—*Unnnhhh*!"

Shayla's demand went unheard after he eased into her from the back. Romeo's sudden entrance was a combination of pleasure and pain due to his massive size. At that moment, protection was the last thing on their minds. "Oh, shit. Don't stop!" Shayla bellowed. Her hand on his leg pleaded for him to not go any deeper.

"Move dat hand," Romeo demanded, gripping her hair tighter.

Shayla wasn't used to being dominated so aggressively; yet it only made her pussy wetter. Deliberately disobeying him, she tried her best to catch his deep strokes. But he was a Taurus who thrived off control.

"You hardheaded I see."

Turning her around to face him, Romeo effortlessly lifted her up and carried her out the shower. He needed to lay her down if he planned on taming her stubborn ass. Once inside the master bedroom, Romeo gently tossed Shayla onto the bed—the same one she had ironically sold him.

Moonlight poured into the room and reflected off his decorative tattoos. Shayla wasn't sure what most of them meant but she was positive some were gang-related.

Slowly, Romeo lowered himself onto the bed. The plush mattress creaked underneath his weight. Like a predator stalking its prey, he crawled over in between Shayla's thighs.

Romeo then pinned one of her legs so far back her toes touched the button-tufted headboard. Before Shayla could brace herself, he plunged deep inside her wetness. Cream glistened on his pole as he grinded rhythmically.

"I don't want you to give dis pussy to no other nigga," Romeo told her. "Can you do that for me, baby?"

"Oh, shit, yes!" Shayla cried out. Tears formed in her eyes from the pleasure. His sex game was amazing.

Romeo was an expert when it came to locating that special spot. As soon as he found

Shayla's he pounded it ferociously until she screamed out his name. The nearest neighbor was half a mile away, but he was sure by now they knew his government.

Overwhelmed with pleasure, Shayla tried to inch away. "Un-unh," he grunted, firmly holding her in place. Women who ran were usually only punished more.

Feeling her walls constricting, Romeo drilled her even harder. Shayla's whimpers bounced off the bedroom walls. He could tell she'd never had a nigga stroke her like he did. Within seconds, Shayla finally exploded in a waterfall of liquid which left her legs shaking.

Gripping the sheets, she shivered in blissful satisfaction. "Oh…my…God," she panted breathlessly. "That was the best sex I've ever had. I…didn't even know I could squirt."

"Who said we was finished?" Romeo asked, flipping her over. "Put dat ass up. We ain't done."

Shayla excitedly did as she was told before burying her head in the nearest silk pillow. She squealed when his thumb slid inside her tight asshole, but strangely it made her pussy wetter. Romeo was doing things to her no man had ever done, and she was hardly ready for a guy like him.

"How you like dat shit?" Romeo asked, slowly stroking her. His curved dick hit her spot perfectly from his angle, and Shayla was close to cumming a second time.

"Oh, shit. What are you doing to me?" she moaned.

Leaning over, Romeo placed a trail of kisses along her spine. Instead of pounding her like he'd been doing, he decided to take his time. And as expected, his patience paid off after Shayla came again.

Unable to hold himself back any longer, Romeo exploded deep inside of Shayla. Usually, he was strapped and never so careless; but she made it hard for a nigga to play by the rules.

Panting heavily, Romeo collapsed beside her. Sweat glistened on his forehead and each abdominal muscle flexed with every breath.

Running a hand through her hair, Shayla turned to face him. She figured now was as good as any to say it. "Um…what do you do?" she asked sheepishly.

His response in return was faint snores.

18

It was a quarter to three when Kim arrived home from grocery shopping. Rita was on her way back from getting Jordan from school, and Kim wanted to have something ready for him to snack on. Just as she was climbing out her Range, a colorful delivery truck pulled in behind her.

"What the hell?"

The driver anxiously hopped out before sliding open the back doors. "Are you Ms. Lopez?" he asked.

Shielding the sun from her eyes, she said, "Yes."

"I just need you to sign for these and I'll be on my way."

Kimberlyn watched as he brought her a beautiful bouquet of Asiatic lilies and roses. Attached to it was a small card. "Wow, these are gorgeous," she smiled. After signing for the flowers, she bid the driver farewell.

Walking back towards the house, Kimberlyn opened the card and read the brief message:

Dinner tonight at 8. Nikolais Roof. Don't be late.

Desmond.

P.S. Hope you like the flowers

Smiling like a little girl with a schoolboy crush, Kimberlyn folded the card closed. Since she wanted to get the groceries in first she placed the bouquet of roses on the porch and grabbed the bags. Sticking her key in the door, she twisted, and pushed it open—

Out of nowhere, a large hand grabbed her face and snatched her inside. The groceries slipped from her hands immediately as she went to defend herself. Unfortunately, her attacker was much stronger than she. Grabbing her roughly, he slammed Kimberlyn against a nearby wall. Tears formed in her eyes when she felt him tug at her jeans.

With her chest pressed against the wall, she couldn't see who the son of a bitch was. Her heart hammered ferociously, and sweat had even begun to form on her head from the tussle.

"GET OFF ME!" Kim screamed, thrashing about.

Pinning his strong body against hers, Kim's attacker snatched her jeans down halfway.

"Please don't this!" she cried, tears streaming down her cheeks. She'd never been so afraid in her life. She would've gladly taken death instead. The only thing Kim was grateful for was her son not being there. "Please, stop!"

Fumbling with his belt, the intruder quickly freed himself. Kim was disgusted when she heard him spit on his hand and lubricate his dick. Without warning, he jammed his rock hard shaft inside.

"Stop! St—*Aaahh, ahhh,*" Kim moaned. The strokes were all too familiar to mistake.

Pinning one of her hands above her head, Cool interlocked their fingers. He made sure to keep his pace slow and steady as he fucked her on the hallway wall. "You miss daddy?" he whispered.

"Cool…*Mmm*…Wait—stop," Kim whimpered. Her mouth said one thing, but her kitty continued to get creamier with each stroke.

"You don't want me to stop," he said, nibbling on her ear.

"Cool…*ooohhh*….shit." Kim shut her eyes tightly, mouth agape. She'd been missing his pipe game for nearly a year, and it was well worth the wait. But as soon as Desmond crept in her mind, she instantly became turned off. "Cool, wait. Hold up."

Instead of doing as she asked, he pumped harder and faster.

"Cool, I said stop!" Kim screamed, shoving him away. Breathing heavily, she stared at her baby daddy in disgust. She couldn't say his early release was a pleasant surprise. Lately, she didn't even feel the same about him.

Cool's dick glistened with her juices as he stood there in confusion. "Wassup?" he asked, slightly annoyed. He had a major backup and Kim was fucking around.

"We need to talk," she said, fixing up her clothes.

"'Bout what?"

"Us…I don't think we should be together right now."

Cool forced a laugh before shaking his head. "Are you kiddin' me? A mufucka been locked up a whole year and that's da bullshit you hit me with?" Angered by the bad news, he put his flaccid dick away and buttoned his jeans. "I thought you would've been happy as fuck to see me. But you obviously still bitter 'bout dat last visit."

Before Kimberly could respond, the front door opened.

"Kim!" Rita called out. "It's some roses here for you on the porch—Damn, girl I almost tripped on these bags—"

Her voice instantly trailed off after seeing Cool standing there in the flesh. His name left her lips in a low whisper. She barely even noticed the spilled groceries on the floor.

Cool wasn't as surprised to see Rita—or his son for that matter. Instead his focus was on the flowers in Rita's hands. "*Roses*? Who da fuck givin' you roses?" he rounded on Kim.

Before she could think of a plausible lie, Cool looked down at her left hand. Kimberlyn wasn't wearing her engagement ring. Sadly, it was still sitting on Desmond's coffee table in his home.

"Cool, I—"

WHAP!

Cool slapped Kimberlyn so hard her head bounced off the picture frame behind her. It shattered instantly upon impact before dropping to the floor.

"*Mommy*!" Jordan cried out.

"YOU BEEN FUCKIN' WHILE I BEEN LOCKED UP, BITCH?!"

Cool's saliva sprayed Kimberlyn's face as he screamed at her like a madman. She wasn't expecting him to go from zero to one hundred so quickly, but she knew he had a temper. Most times Cool gave her the benefit of the doubt. However, that time he didn't even give her a chance to explain herself.

"Oh, my God! Jordan, go to your room!" Rita said, shooing him away. Since a baby, she'd tried to shield him from the violence of his parents' relationship.

Jordan didn't budge, and Rita had no time to make him as she ran over to help. "What is your problem? Get your hands off my niece!" She made a move to grab Cool's arm, but he violently snatched away.

"Bitch, unless you gon' help her find dat mufuckin' ring I suggest you raise up out my face!"

"Aunt Rita, it's okay," Kim said in her defense. Cool putting his hands on her was one thing, but she couldn't have him assaulting her 57-year old aunt.

"It's not okay!" Rita snapped.

Cool clenched his fists as a warning, and she instantly got the hint. Fearful of what he'd do to a withered old lady, Rita finally backed up.

Looking back over at his fiancé, Cool pointed a thick finger in her face. "I'ma ask ya ass one mo' time," he said through clenched teeth. "You been fuckin' while I been locked up?"

Everyone held their breaths as they waited for Kim's response. Unfortunately, her silence said it all.

Stricken with rage, Cool snatched her up by her hair and dragged her towards their bedroom. He didn't want Jordan to see the ass whupping he was about to inflict on his mother.

There were tears in Cool's eyes as he pushed Kimberlyn inside the bedroom. "Everything I did was for you! And in turn yo' ass couldn't even be loyal!"

"Cool, please let me explain—"

Kim's sentence was cut short after a brutal slap that left her dazed. Losing her balance, she fell backwards on the king sized bed. She could taste blood in her mouth, and she hated that her gun was so far away.

"This mothafuckin' house you sleep in, I brought! Them mothafuckin' clothes you wear, I got'chu! That expensive ass private school dat lil' nigga go to, I pay for! Bitch, I took yo' ass out the gutter and polished you, and this is how you repay me?! You couldn't even wait for a nigga!"

"Get the fuck out my house!" Kim screamed. "My name is on the papers! GET THE FUCK OUT!" Her entire front row of teeth was covered in blood. Cool had really done a number on her being heavy-handed as he was.

Cool was just about to pounce on her ass when Rita barged inside the bedroom. "I'm calling the police!" she said with her cellphone to her ear. She may not have been able to fight Cool off, but she sure as hell knew who could.

At that moment, Cool was faced with the choice of going back to jail or ringing Kim's neck. The latter sounded more enticing, but prison was a hellhole he never wanted to return to. Now that he was free, he wanted to keep it that way.

Reluctantly, Cool backed off before backpedaling out the room. “Fuck out my way,” he sneered at Rita. In the hallway, he punched a massive hole in the wall which made Jordan cry.

Stumbling out the bed, Kimberlyn went after him. Not even fear could stop her from uttering her two cents. “Don’t you ever bring yo’ ass back here!” she screamed. Blood leaked down her chin and splattered onto the hardwood floors.

Stopping at the front door, Cool turned on his heels. “If you think you gon’ fill my slot wit’ dat nigga, you got another thing comin’! Bitch, I’ll kill a mufucka ‘fore I see dat happen!”

Rita kept her finger hovering over the nine on her keypad as she watched Cool leave. Although he took care of them, she had never been his biggest fan for the way he treated Kim. After today, she despised him wholeheartedly.

“I can’t believe I ever did shit for this nigga!” Kim said, wiping her bloodied mouth. “Risking my freedom for that mothafucka. I’m done! You hear me, Cool?!” she screamed out the doorway. “DONE!”

“We’ll see,” Cool said, climbing inside his 2013 Acura.

***

It was ten minutes to five when Romeo and two of his closest patnas pulled into the over capitated lot of *Planet Fitness.* Unbeknownst to Shayla, he planned on paying Dexter a little visit while on the clock. He also had a few choice words for him as well.

That day he was riding in the big boy toy; a custom bronze 2014 Hummer. Anytime his niggas rolled with him to handle business, he pulled the truck out. Today was no different. Unlike Desmond, Romeo didn't mind getting his hands a little dirty. Oftentimes his boy lectured him about that shit, but Romeo was born into the Piru life, and some bad habits were hard to break.

Hopping out the Hummer, he and his goons swaggered towards the entrance. Once inside, Romeo headed straight to the customer service desk. "Aye, I'm lookin' for somebody named Dexter," he told the male employee. "I need to holla at him 'bout some business right quick."

Believing the question was fitness related, he said, "The last time I saw him he was in the locker room," He then pointed in the direction.

"'Preciate it," Romeo told him.

Without hesitation, he and his people made their way towards the locker room. Inside were two guys, but for some reason Romeo automatically knew who Dexter was. Tapping his nigga, Romeo gestured for him to get rid of the lone eyewitness.

Not wanting any trouble, the member quickly fled from the room. Dexter, however, was totally unaware of his fate as he stood with his back to Romeo. He had just closed his locker door when he turned around and saw three suspicious men standing there.

"Aye, you Dex?" Romeo asked him.

Dexter glanced from Romeo to the goons standing behind him. They had trouble written all over their faces, and they definitely didn't look like they needed fitness counseling. Even though he was somewhat intimidated Dexter stood his ground. "Shit, who wanna know?"

Romeo looked over at his patna who was eagerly waiting for the cue. They lived for violence so they had no problem getting buck.

"So I take it you da one puttin' hands on Shayla," Romeo said, giving him a second chance to come correct.

After hearing his ex's name, Dexter immediately broke out laughing. The fact that he wasn't taking them seriously was extremely insulting. Unfortunately, he couldn't see the red flags hanging out their back pockets. All three of them were about that life.

"Mufucka, you really came up to my job over a bitch?" Dexter spat. "I should put my hands on *yo'* ass—"

Before he could finish, Romeo charged Dexter and slammed him against the lockers. Though Dexter was an inch taller and incredibly fit, Romeo was much stronger. With rage in his eyes, he hemmed Dexter up like he was some chump nigga in the streets. It wasn't even about Shayla anymore. Now it was simply about respect.

"Fuck nigga, I should break yo' weak ass!" Romeo said through clenched teeth. "The only reason I'm givin' yo' ass da benefit of da doubt is 'cuz you Shayla's people. But if I ever see or hear about you puttin' yo' hands on her, we gon' have a serious mufuckin' problem. Ya feel me?"

"Aight, bruh. Got damn," Dexter huffed, unable to move. Romeo's forearm was pressed firmly against his throat, blocking his airway passage. Bowing down was his only way to ensure he lived.

Reluctantly, Romeo let Dexter go. The look in his eyes showed he wasn't afraid to kill, and now Shayla's ex knew it. Massaging his throat, Dexter watched the three men walk towards the exit.

"You might think you know her," he said after them. "But you don't. 'Cuz if you did you'd know you wasn't even her type. But it's cool." Dexter laughed sadistically. "I'ma just watch ya'll crash and burn. I'll be there to pick up the pieces afterwards."

One of Romeo's boys made a move to go back but he stopped him. No bitch was worth fighting over. But as far as Dexter putting his hands on Shayla it was a wrap for that shit.

"We made our point," Romeo said. "Dis mufucka ain't 'een worth it, bruh." Together, they exited the locker room as quickly as they'd come.

"Aye, I'll set my stopwatch, bruh!" Dexter called out, laughing hysterically.

19

Later on that evening, Cool found himself at a local sports bar to blow off some steam. Had it not been for him having one foot in and one foot out the system, Cool would've broken Kim's neck.

This bitch walkin' 'round town without a ring like she cute and shit. I'ma show that hoe better than I can tell her though. First thing tomorrow, Cool planned on shutting off every utility in her home. The house may have been in her name but all the bills were in his. Kim had another thing coming if she thought he was going to let another nigga benefit from his hard work.

Sitting at the bar alone, Cool nursed a beer and shot of Hennessey. Bitter and hateful thoughts clouded his mind, and all he wanted to do was hurt his fiancé. He didn't give a damn about hurting his son too in the process.

Every so often, Cool glanced at the door each time a person walked in. Since he'd been running his mouth to the law, he was naturally paranoid. Motherfuckers who leaked info usually didn't last very long in the streets. Cool's pride wouldn't permit him to go into protective custody. He figured he was a big boy who could take care of himself. Even though he was out on parole, Cool kept a strap on like a dyke. Nobody was going to catch him slipping.

Brewing in his own malevolent thoughts, Cool barely noticed the beautiful woman walking inside the bar. It was the intoxicating scent of her Chanel perfume that caused him to look up.

"Damn," he mumbled, eyeing the length of her body.

Shawty looked foreign but was built like a sister. Ironically, that was exactly how Cool liked his women.

Keeping his gaze locked on her, he watched her take a seat at the end of the bar. Tossing her hair over her shoulder, she beckoned for the bartender. Her air of assertiveness made Cool automatically think she was a woman in charge. Yet the fact that she was having a drink alone said so much more.

Cool waited ten minutes to see if she was waiting on a friend. When it was apparent that she was solo-dolo, he smoothly slid out his seat and approached her. On his way, he gestured to the bartender to get them a second round on him.

Thankfully, Cool had a little cushion cash—that Kim didn't know about. That night, he planned to binge on alcohol and drugs. But doing that shit alone was no fun. Most of his homeboys were probably getting their rights read at that very moment thanks to him. So making new—preferably female—associates was definitely in order.

"'Scuse me, Miss Lady," Cool spoke up. "Can I join you?"

Ava flashed a million dollar smile. The flirtatious look in her eyes let him know that she liked what she saw. “I don’t know,” she teases. “Can you?”

20

Two Weeks Later

Shayla begrudgingly headed towards the entrance of Atlanta's popular mega club, *The Mansion Elan*. Dressed in her best, she had only come out because Kimberlyn begged her to. For the last couple weeks, she'd been keeping herself cooped in the house, depressed that Romeo had dropped her like a bad habit.

In spite of the wonderful two days they spent together, he never called Shayla afterwards. She'd even gone out her way to hit him up a few times. But when it was obvious that he was avoiding her, she quickly backed off. The last thing Shayla wanted was to seem like a pest. Still, she couldn't stop herself from believing he was an asshole.

Romeo fell into her world, rewarded her with the best sex of her life, and then seemingly vanished. *If he only wanted some pussy, I would've rather he been honest*. She'd take a real nigga over a car any day.

Sashaying inside the building, Shayla tried her best to put on her game face. She'd been being pretty elusive the last few days, and she owed her girl a good time.

Once inside, Shayla found Kimberlyn in a reserved VIP section. "Hey, bitch," Kim waved excitedly. She looked extremely vibrant, and there was a natural glow to her skin. Shayla could tell there was someone special in Kim's life making her happy. She never seemed so bubbly.

Shayla had no idea Cool was out, and Kim didn't plan on bringing it up. In her book, he was a done deal and all she wanted to do was get on with her life.

After the altercation with her baby daddy, she temporarily backed off Desmond for a second to get her mind right. Cool had her all fucked up in the head. Yet there was also a part of her afraid to start over with someone new—especially someone who had their own share of baggage.

Shaking off her reservations, Kim went on and took that chance. So far Desmond was everything she wanted in a man. He was sweet, charming, funny, and generous. When Cool went on a petty ass rampage, and turned off her utilities, Desmond cut them all back on with no problem. Most of all Desmond made Kim feel secure, protected. With a relentless baby daddy who knew no limits, it was good to have someone strong and ready in her corner.

"You look cute," Kim smiled, looking her friend over.

Shayla was dressed for the Gawds in a nude strapless exotic print skirt and gold single sole heels. Her hair was pinned up, showing off her high cheekbone structure. Her makeup was subtle and neutral, and there wasn't a flaw in sight.

"So do you mamas," Shayla laughed.

Kimberlyn wore a shimmery tight-fitting gray dress which cost more than her mortgage. Prior to the event, Desmond surprised her with a bag from *Nordstroms*.

"When'd you get here?" Shayla yelled over the loud music.

"About five minutes ago."

Shayla was just about to ask Kim where she got her shoes when she noticed a familiar face through the thick of the crowd.

Romeo.

An unsettling feeling immediately took over Shayla after seeing him booed up with a cute redbone. Him, Desmond, and their entire camp were parked a few sections down from them.

Secretly, it hurt Shayla to see him having such a good time. She'd thought they had made a connection, but it was obvious Romeo only wanted to play mind games.

From the very beginning, he'd given Shayla the impression that he was a male-hoe, but she still allowed high hopes. *I should've known better*, she told herself.

Kimberlyn looked over her shoulder to see what had Shayla so captivated.

"Did you know he was gonna be here?" Shayla asked. She was feeling some type of way and Kim knew it.

"Well…I mean—yeah. Desmond invited me to his friend Ava's birthday party. So I invited you," Kimberlyn explained. "But I didn't know ya'll wasn't kicking it like that."

Like Kim, Shayla too had her own secrets she wasn't clamoring to share. No one wanted to admit they had been shitted on.

"Forget about it. It's not a big deal," Shayla waved her off. She wasn't going to let Romeo ruin her evening.

"You sure?" There was a genuine look of concern on Kim's face.

"Yeah, I'm good," Shayla lied. Truth be told, she was fuming inside. There was nothing she wanted to do more than toss a drink in his face. *Nigga ain't shit.*

All of a sudden, Kim's girl Nina walked up waving excitedly. "What up, babe?" she sang. "Thanks for the invite. Long time no see. Yo' ass been MIA lately. Either Cool got out or a new nigga got you locked down."

Shayla didn't think it was possible for her night to get any worse. She couldn't stand Nina's ass. She was so over the top with everything—including her outfit for that night. Her black mesh two piece left little to the imagination; but that was the typical dress code of a thot.

Shayla did an automatic double take at the guy standing behind Nina. It was her ex, Dexter.

"Yeah, I been kickin' it," Kim said sheepishly. "And I see you been too." Her entire disposition changed after seeing Nina with Shayla's ex-boyfriend. Although Nina and Shay weren't the best of friends they still were cordial with each other. In Kim's opinion, Nina was definitely breaking the girl code.

Nina looked back at Dexter and smiled flirtatiously. "Yeah, something like that." She then looked over at Shayla as if she dared her to say something.

Dexter looked extremely uncomfortable, but he stood his ground.

"Anyway, we'll be back. A bitch need a drink." With that said, Nina grabbed Dex's hand and proceeded to walk off.

"*You invited them*?" Shayla hissed. "Did you know Nina was seeing my ex?"

Nina was barely two feet away when she heard her name. Stopping in her tracks, she turned around to see if there was something that needed to be addressed.

"I invited Nina, but I didn't know she was gonna show up with Dex. Hell, I'm just as shocked as you," Kimberlyn said in her defense.

"*Really*?" Shayla asked, growing angrier. "'Cuz to me it looks like you had some ulterior motives when you invited me!"

"Shayla, boo. You really need to calm down. You trippin'," Kim said. Her girl was doing way too much, and it took everything to keep her patience.

"Um…Did I hear my name?" Nina asked with sarcasm in her tone.

"Bitch, go GPS the nearest seat! I'm not talkin' to yo' ass!"

Kimberlyn's eyes popped open in surprise. She wasn't used to seeing Shayla get buck. She was always so calm and reserved. However, everyone had a breaking point.

"I don't give a fuck! I'm hearing my name ringing though!" Nina clapped back.

"Aye, chill, Nina," Dexter said, trying to pull her back.

Kimberlyn quickly stood in front Shayla. "Boo, calm down. It ain't even that serious," she told her friend.

"It sure ain't. You da only one bothered sweetie. Please believe we sleep peacefully at night. Get one, hoe!"

"You fucking bitch!" Shayla screamed. Reaching around Kim, she snatched a handful of Nina's hair.

Upon hearing all the commotion, Romeo looked over at Shayla and Kim's section. It was his first time noticing she was in the club. What he didn't expect was to see her turning up.

Desmond quickly rushed over to help his girl out. They were wildin' and creating a huge scene in the club.

Luckily, Dexter was able to pry Shayla's hand loose while Desmond pulled the girls apart.

"You wanna hit me, bitch?! Hit me!" Nina said, kicking and screaming. A breast had popped out of place, but she hardly seemed to notice or care.

"Suck sick dick, bitch! You triflin' as fuck and you know it! You fuckin' backdoor hoe!" Shayla hollered. She was acting completely out of character. Romeo and Dexter had her head and heart all messed up.

"Bitch, I'll be a backdoor hoe with yo' nigga though!" Nina yelled.

Dexter struggled to drag Nina away from the altercation. She always did have a big mouth, but she sucked a nigga into submission so he put up with her ass.

It took both Desmond and Kimberlyn to hold Shayla back. She didn't calm down until Nina was finally out of site.

Back in her section, Ava rolled her eyes in irritation. Tonight was her special day and Kim and her ratchet ass friend were ruining it. She also despised the fact Kimberlyn was able to easily steal Desmond's attention from her.

Jealousy coursed through Ava's veins as she stormed out the VIP and to the restroom. After locking herself in an empty stall, she plopped down on the toilet seat and ran a hand through her hair.

Fuck Desmond. He's so damn blind to not realize he's got a good thing right here. Ava didn't know why Desmond kept going for the same type of chicks. All of them had the same outcome.

"I didn't even invite that bitch," Ava complained. Her mood was now sour and it had a lot to do with Dez's new girl.

Digging in her clutch, Ava extracted a small sandwich bag. Cool had turned her out to the powerful drug, and after her first hit she was addicted. She and Cool had been going hard together the last couple weeks, and while he was fun and exciting her heart was still with Desmond.

For years, Ava had hoped and prayed he'd eventually break up with his BM. And even after he did she still stalled for another six months. Now

Kimberlyn was in the picture, making shit even harder.

I am so fucking stupid, Ava cursed herself. *I should've said something when I had the chance.* She was losing it, and she didn't even know it. Desmond had her head gone and the recreational drug use was only making it worse.

Why should I sit back and let these bitches have him?

Bitter with regret, Ava dumped a small amount of coke on her hand and sniffed it off.

Outside in the club, Shayla and Kimberlyn continued with their banter.

"Shay, you hype as hell tonight. This ain't even you, boo. Why don't you have a drink or something? Mellow out a lil'—"

"I don't wanna drink!" Shayla snapped. "I wanna know why you ain't tell me your *friend* was fucking my ex! I would've never kept some shit like that from you. And you got the nerve to call a bitch like that yo' girl?! If she'd do some shit like that to me, she'd do some shit like that to you!"

Kim tried to laugh Shayla off. "Girl, you talking crazy. And instead of jumpin' off at me and Nina you should've been checkin' Dexter's ass."

"Don't tell me what I should've done," Shayla said. "*You* shouldn't have invited me to this bullshit ass party tonight! My mama always said a stranger will stab you in the front but a friend will stab you in the back. You two bitches deserve each other."

Brushing past Kimberlyn, Shayla quickly left the VIP section. She'd never felt so embarrassed in her life. Shayla tried her best to avoid stares as she shuffled through the crowd of partygoers. She was just about to leave the club until she remembered Romeo was there.

Fuck it. I'm already on one, she told herself. Turning around, she headed to his section.

21

"Can I talk to you?"

Shayla didn't have the least amount of consideration when she barged inside Romeo's VIP section. The redbone sitting next to him looked Shayla up and down with disgust. She was two seconds from putting her ass in her place. She'd earned her place that evening, and would be damned if she let Shayla have it.

"Why?" Romeo asked nastily. "I saw you over there wildin'. Don't bring that messy shit over here."

Shayla couldn't believe Romeo was openly dissing her in front of his peers. When they were kicking it, he made her feel so special. Now he was making her feel like total shit. Unable to back down, Shayla continued with her piece.

"I…I thought—"

"You thought what?" Romeo interrupted. "'Cuz you mopped me down you was my bitch? I got'chu a whip. I ain't get you no ring. Fuck outta here. I ain't that nigga."

Romeo's groupie broke out laughing at Shayla's expense. She felt lower than low. Never had a guy talked to her so recklessly.

Refusing to let them see her tears fall, Shayla walked out the VIP fuming mad. She could feel the waterworks coming as she headed towards the exit.

"All dat shit wasn't necessary, bruh," Desmond said. He had just walked up when he overheard Romeo going in on Shayla. He'd never condoned the way Romeo treated chicks, but Shayla was good peoples. "Why you do her like dat? To hurt her?"

Romeo took a swig straight from a Hennessey bottle. "Nah. To protect her," he said. Shayla was better off without a nigga like him in her life. She'd only get hurt in the end from having her hopes too high. He was a hood nigga who put cash before commitment. In his mind, a bitch would only slow him down. So he used them for what they were worth and kept it moving.

Desmond gave his boy the side eye. "Fuck that. I think you tryin' to protect yaself…"

Meanwhile, halfway across the club, Shayla was stopped by Dexter on her way out. "Hold up, Shay. Can we talk?"

"Go talk to your bitch! We don't have shit to discuss."

"I think we do," Dexter told her. "'Cuz if we didn't you wouldn't have started spazzin' when you saw me with Nina. You still got feelings for a nigga."

"Boy, she can have your ass!" Shayla spat. "Let's start there. Get over your damn self!"

Before Dexter could respond, Romeo walked up and grabbed Shayla's free hand. "Aye, we gotta rap," he said.

Right there in the middle of the club, both men played tug-of-war with Shayla. Territorial over his girl, Dexter pulled Shayla towards him. Romeo may've got at him in the locker room, but he wasn't going to let that happen tonight. His pride was on the line.

Angered by Dexter's boldness, Romeo practically snatched Shayla from him. She nearly lost her balance in her heels; and she had to grab him to keep from falling.

"I think you better fall back, homie," Romeo threatened. The menacing look in his eyes was enough to make Dexter let go. He could play if he wanted to. Romeo had no problem paying to make his ass go missing.

Holding his hands up in mock surrender, Dexter looked from Shayla to Romeo. "Aight then. You got it, bro'."

"Yeah, I know I do," Romeo said, looking him up and down. "You just make sure you know dat shit too."

As soon as Dexter walked off, Shayla snatched away from Romeo. "What fucking game are you playing at?!" she yelled. "You don't want me but you don't want nobody else to have me? What type of shit is that?"

"Shayla, lemme explain—"

"You don't need to," she said. "You showed me with your actions."

Shayla left his ass standing in the middle of the club when walked out and headed towards her car. The breeze outside was refreshing considering the fact that she was burning mad inside. Tears stung Shayla's eyes, but she tried her best to keep them from falling. She didn't want to see another man for a whole two months. They all were pieces of shit.

Stopping at her car, Shayla froze in place. She was an emotional wreck that night. "I should've never let a couple guys get me out my hookup," she told herself.

"Shayla?" Romeo called out from behind.

Teary-eyed, she turned around to face him. Suddenly, all Shayla saw was red as she walked up and slapped him. The momentum made the blunt tucked behind his ear fall.

"How dare you disrespect me in front of those people!" she screamed.

Romeo casually bent down and picked up his blunt. He decided to let Shayla have it since he knew that shit was coming. “You gon’ yell at me or you gon’ talk to me?” he asked calmly.

“Fuck you!” was all Shayla could think to say.

Without warning, Romeo snatched her ass up and pulled her close. She wanted to be angry with him, but his aggression was such a turn on. “Let me go,” she said, wriggling in his embrace. Secretly, she didn’t want him to.

Ignoring her useless demands, Romeo backed Shayla up against her Benz. “I don’t think I wanna do that.” Staring deep in her mahogany eyes, he almost became lost in them.

“Go tell that to your groupie in the club,” Shayla said, still on her petty rant.

Romeo wasn’t fazed by her jealousy. It actually showed him that she really was feeling a nigga. Leaning in, he stole a kiss regardless of Shayla being angry. Although she tried to fight it in the beginning, she quickly melted into his strong embrace. Romeo was so damn irresistible, and Shayla despised her body for betraying her.

“Don’t worry about her,” Romeo whispered after they pulled apart. “She where she needs to be and you where you need to be.”

Shayla couldn’t argue with his statement.

"Come on, let's get in da whip," Romeo said. "We doin' the most out here right now. And I hate for mufuckas to be in my bizness."

Wiping her tears away, Shayla hit the automatic door unlock. Together they climbed inside and sat in silence for a few minutes.

Firing up his blunt, Romeo took a few puffs before releasing the smoke through his nostrils. Jhene Aiko's "*3:16*" played softly through the speakers.

"I'm not gon' sit here and flex like ya heart's safe wit' a nigga like me," Romeo began. "Hell, I'ma just keep it real." There was a small pause as he thought about what he was going to say next. "But if you can work with me, I'm ridin' with you, Shayla. And I ain't ever told no female that," he added.

Shayla sniffled and grinned. "So that's supposed to make me feel special?" she asked sarcastically.

Romeo was happy to see a glimmer of happiness on her face. "You are," he told her. "Come here…"

Unfastening her seatbelt, Shayla slowly leaned over and kissed him.

I do not feel the fear of falling…I wanna fly…

If it all goes well, then I will...But what if I don't?

I'll be right where I was before...But I'm not alone...

You say "take my hand"...And we go...

And I hope that we don't overdose...

Jhene Aiko crooned in the background as the two indulged in a passionate make-up kiss. Feeling her temperature slowly rising, Shayla crawled out her seat and mounted Romeo. He wasted no time lifting her dress up and pulling her panties to the side.

Shayla anxiously unbuttoned his jeans before pulling his rod free. Locking their lips, she slowly eased down on top of him. "I wanna know everything about you," she said in between kisses.

"Shit…you will…" Shayla was so warm and wet upon his entrance; she had that gushy. "I'ma tell you erything," Romeo groaned. Reclining his head, all he wanted Shayla to do was take control. Even the wildest of dogs could be tamed.

22

"You holla'd at ya girl?" Desmond asked the following afternoon.

He and Kim were seated on a bench at a local park while watching Jordan play. Over the last few days, the two had gotten incredibly close. The more Cool faded into the background, the more Desmond slowly took over. It had actually gotten to a point where Kim rarely if ever thought about her ex-fiancé.

"Not yet," she sighed. "I hit her up a few times this morning, but she ain't answer."

"Give her a few days to chill. She'll be straight," Desmond promised. From where he sat, he could see Jordan playing tag with another young boy. "Damn…I always wanted a son."

Kim laughed. "Maybe you'll get one, one day."

Desmond nudged her playfully. "You gon' gimme one?"

"Boy, bye," Kim smiled.

After composing himself, Desmond continued. "Anyway, I been thinkin'," he began. "Why don't you let me move you and J into somethin' bigger? I mean ya'll crib straight and all, but more space wouldn't hurt."

Honestly, Desmond just wanted her closer to him. And he hated visiting a home that her ex put her in.

Kim drew back and looked at Desmond like he was crazy. "Listen at you trying to spoil me."

"I wanna spoil the fuck outta you," he said.

Kim's smile slowly vanished as she looked deep in his eyes. "How 'bout you start by telling me what you do for a living?" There was no trace of humor in her tone when she spoke. "I know you ain't working a regular nine to five."

"Why can't I be?" Desmond asked curiously.

"You never took me as a nine-to-five type of nigga," Kim answered. "Just be real. Are you involved in something dangerous? Something me and Jordan could possibly be exposed to? 'Cuz I ain't really trying to have my son around no bullshit. And I ain't trying to get caught up in none either. I just closed that chapter in my life and I don't wanna reopen it."

Desmond sighed deeply before running a hand over his brush waves. He knew the question was going to pop up sooner or later. With the boss-like way he was living it was bound to come. Desmond only hoped it was later rather than sooner.

"Aight…I do sell a lil' bit of weed," he admitted. "But I ain't mixed up in no shit that could get you hurt. I keep my nose clean. You can believe that. I'd never endanger you and ya kid, feel me?"

"Okay," Kim said earnestly. Although she respected Desmond for telling the truth, she feared losing him the same way she had lost Cool; to prison.

"You trust me?" Desmond asked her.

"…I do…," Kim confessed. "I probably shouldn't. But I do."

***

Jordan was fast asleep when Kimberlyn and Desmond pulled into her driveway. He'd tuckered himself out at the playground, and was out for the count.

"You want me to carry him inside?" Desmond offered, turning off the engine.

Before Kimberlyn could respond, a wooden bat suddenly slammed into the back window.

23

KKSSSHHHHHH!

Glass sprayed onto Jordan, instantly waking him. A small piece nicked his cheek, but his safety was the least of Dana's worries.

"Get out the car, mothafucka!" she screamed.

Kimberlyn and Desmond hopped out simultaneously. Kim rushed to tend to Jordan while Desmond went to calm Dana.

"Aye, what the fuck is you doin'?!" he barked.

Dana took a wild swing at Desmond's head but missed. "I told yo' ass to get rid of these hoes!" she hollered.

Enraged that her son was harmed, Kim charged at Dana like a madwoman. In an attempt to defend herself, she swung the wooden bat with force. Kim's arm automatically went up to protect her face. Fortunately, it took the blow instead of her skull. With adrenaline coursing through her blood, Kim barely felt it as she attacked Dana.

Blow for blow, she wailed on the baby mama from hell until she finally saw blood drop. "You fucking bitch!" Kim growled repeatedly.

Thankfully, Desmond managed to pull Kim off before she killed Dana. His baby mama's nose was bloodied by the time Kimberlyn finished with her.

"Kim, chill!" Desmond ordered. "Go get Jordan and take him in the house!"

Panting heavily, Kimberlyn looked from Dana to Desmond. Had it not been for her son needing medical attention she would've gladly went for a round two.

"Your bitch is outta line! I want her off my fucking property!" Kim screamed. Mumbling a few choice words, she headed to the car and collected Jordan. He was still crying when she carried him to the house.

"Man, what da fuck is you doin', Dana?" Desmond snapped. He couldn't believe he'd carelessly allowed things to get to that point. Dana talked a lot of shit, but he had underestimated her actions. As a matter of fact, Desmond thought she had grown tired and went back to Cali. Unfortunately, he was wrong. Dana was only waiting for the perfect moment swoop in and attack.

Tears streamed down her cheeks as she stood in front of Desmond. Dana looked a hot mess with her hair in disarray and nose leaking. Desmond was the love of her life, and she couldn't accept losing him to another. Usually, Dana was never that violent, but desperate times called for desperate measure.

"You promised me you wasn't gon' let the money change you!" she cried.

"I didn't change! YOU DID!" Desmond spat. "Look what da fuck you doin' right now! You need to accept we over—"

"WE AIN'T OVER!" Dana screamed. "It ain't over 'til I say it's over. I got all the time in the world, Desmond. I can do this shit everyday all day."

"You really fuckin' trippin'," he said, shaking his head. "And where my mufuckin' daughter at? Answer me dat shit."

Dana stalled with her response, nervously shifting from one foot to the other.

"Where's Destiny? I ain't 'bout to ask you again."

"At the hotel—"

Dana's sentence was cut short after she was violently yoked up. She didn't even get a chance to add that she was with Monica. "Bitch, you got my daughter at a hotel while you out here wildin'?! I should snap yo' fuckin' neck!"

"Get off me!" Dana screamed, snatching away. In the process, Desmond's fingernails scratched into her skin, leaving long sharp gashes in her flesh.

Suddenly, Kim burst through the front door with a loaded 9mm. Standing behind her, Aunt Rita pleaded with her to think reasonably.

Kim wasn't trying to hear that shit as she approached them. Slowly raising the gun, she aimed it directly at Dana.

24

Cool had taken Kim to shooting practice on the regular so her aim was impeccable. If she squeezed, she wouldn't miss.

Desmond quickly jumped in front of Dana to protect her. "Whoa! Whoa! Kim, what da fuck is you doin'?!"

"Tell this crazy bitch to get off my property!" Kim demanded.

"*I'm crazy*?" Dana laughed wickedly. "You the one with the fucking gun!"

"And you the one with the damn bat! And you hurt my son. I should put one between yo' mothafuckin' eyes—"

"Kim, gimme da gun," Desmond ordered. There wasn't a hint of fear on his face as he held his hand out. "I can't let you shoot my baby moms. That's fam."

His comment instantly seared Kim's heart, and cut deep. "Well, you and yo' *fam* can get the fuck off my property!" she countered.

Desmond was shocked by her hostile response. "Damn…like that?" he asked in disbelief.

Unblinkingly, Kim cocked the gun. She wanted both their asses to know she wasn't fucking around. "Just like that."

***

That morning Shayla awoke to soft tapping on her bedroom door.

"Shayla?" Tina called out. "You've got company."

Snatching the sheets off her body, she anxiously sat up in bed. *Romeo*.

Shayla quickly hopped out the full-sized bed and raced to her adjoined bathroom. After speed-gargling with Listerine, she hand-combed through her hair and opened her bedroom door.

Padding barefoot, Shayla headed towards the front of the house. She couldn't believe Romeo had surprised her with a visit. Although he seemed spontaneous enough, she didn't expect him to be so bold. After all, it wasn't like Tina hadn't already expressed her dislike.

To Shayla's dismay, her visitor wasn't the handsome, enigmatic Romeo. Instead, sitting casually on the arm of the sofa in the living room was none other than Dexter.

“What are you doing here?” Shayla asked in a nasty tone.

“I wanted to be able to talk to you without ya boyfriend lurkin’ around.”

Just then Tina walked up and handed Dexter a mug of coffee. She was really reaching with her hospitality since she wanted the two back together.

“I don’t like that cat, Shayla. He’s ignorant as hell. He’s arrogant. And he’s violent. And to be real, I ain’t cool with you kickin’ it with him—”

“Don’t even go there,” Shayla warned Dexter. “Or else you’ll be the biggest hypocrite I know. And why the hell do you even care so much who I’m seeing. From the looks of things, you’ve already moved on. You shouldn’t even be standing in my house right now—”

“Shayla, why are you being so hostile?” Tina butted in. “Listen to the man. In spite of what ya’ll are going through he loves you, and he knows you,” she argued. “We don’t know a damn thing about *Romeo* other than him being a sleaze ball. One day he’s buying you cars and the next he’s avoiding you. I know that type of man. He only wants to control you,” Tina explained. “You may not talk to me much about your dating life, but I see what goes on around you, Shayla. And I have a bad feeling about that one.”

“Okay, ma, first of all, I’m a grown woman,” Shayla retaliated. “I don’t need your acceptance or permission on who to love—”

“*Love*?!” Dexter looked pained by that revelation.

Shayla was just about to correct herself when she felt a bout of nausea wash over her. Sprinting to the nearest bathroom, she dropped down on her knees and vomited uncontrollably.

Tina quickly rushed to her daughter’s aid. But as soon as she realized what was happening she folded her arms in disgust. “Oh Lord. Don’t tell me you went and got pregnant by that fool.”

***

Kimberlyn was washing dishes when she heard faint knocks on the front door. Believing that it was Desmond, she hesitated with answering it. It had only been a few hours since the fiasco with his baby mama occurred, and it was far too early to make amends. Kim needed some space from him and his ‘emotionally unstable baggage’

“You want me to get it?!” Rita called from the den.

Wiping her hands, Kimberlyn turned off the faucets. “No. I got it.” After tossing the dish rag on the counter, she headed to the front door.

Standing on her tiptoes, Kim peered through the peephole. A low sigh immediately left her lips.

She couldn't say she was all too surprised to see him.

Going against her better judgment, Kimberlyn slowly opened the front door. "What do you want, Cool?" she asked unenthusiastically.

Kimberlyn didn't miss the distinguished hickie on his neck. However, she was too beat down mentally to question him about it. Besides, who was she to check Cool about kicking it with someone new? She had Desmond. And Cool was free to do as he pleased as far as Kim was concerned.

Holding up a bag of food from *Benihana's*, Christopher "Cool" Williams offered a gold-fanged grin. "A lil' bit of ya time, babe."

25

Pop a couple bands with a nigga like me...

Loving ain't the same with a nigga like me...

You use to them but ain't no loving me...

I hear what you would say and, girl, it's clear to see...

You should just drink a couple drinks with a nigga like me...

You probably go insane with a nigga like me...

Let's just party till we can't, ain't no loving me...

And I'm the one to blame, ain't no loving me...

So don't come looking for love...

Shayla twiddled with her thumbs as she watched Romeo from where she stood. All day she had contemplated on rather she should tell him she was pregnant or not. By the time 9 pm rolled around, she'd finally come up with a decision. But seeing him there in the flesh had her having doubts.

About a week ago, Romeo had purchased Club XTC from its previous owner. The small hole-in-the-wall establishment was the perfect setting to trap out of while still keeping a low profile. It also made for a great front.

Romeo was completely oblivious to Shayla's presence as he got a lap dance from one of his girls. August Alsina's "*No Love*" poured through the club's massive speakers, and colorful strobe lights reflected off the dancers on stage.

Since it was early there weren't many guests inside. But the few people who were there looked like they were on chill mode.

Prior to arriving, Shayla had texted Romeo letting him know that they needed to talk. He responded with an address on where she could meet him, and twenty minutes later she was there. Stalling and unsure if she should even tell Romeo the truth.

From the way he was entranced by the brown-skinned vixen in his lap, Shayla knew he wasn't ready for commitment. And if he wasn't ready for commitment, he certainly wasn't ready to be a father.

I should just turn around and leave, Shayla thought. *He ain't ready for this life and quite frankly I'm not either.*

Shayla was just about to walk out the club when Romeo suddenly noticed her. Hopping out the red suede chair, he immediately went after her. "Aye, what's up? Where you goin'?" Romeo asked, gently grabbing Shayla's wrist.

"I—I shouldn't…I think it might've been a mistake coming here," Shayla stammered. She didn't even feel like telling him the truth anymore. She just wanted to handle it on her own so they could go their separate ways.

Romeo scoffed lightly. "Why? What's up? Talk to me."

Shayla looked around at their surroundings and frowned. "This really isn't the place, Romeo."

"I know you ain't feelin' some type of way 'bout some strippers," he said. He and Shayla weren't even official, so in his opinion it shouldn't have been an issue. It was nothing more unattractive to Romeo than a female with insecurities.

"It's not that," Shayla said, growingly annoyed. "Look, I—never mind. I should just go." She turned to walk away again but Romeo quickly grabbed her wrist. "Get your damn hands off me! Go back to groping your whores!" Shayla yelled.

Offended by her snappiness, Romeo tossed her hand. "Fuck you then. Get yo' ass up outta here if you don't wanna see it." With that said, he turned and walked off. Shayla was tripping and he didn't have time for that shit. "Bougie ass bitch," he mumbled.

Shayla quickly left the club feeling both disappointed and embarrassed. She started to chalk it as a loss but decided to give herself a couple hours to calm down. After driving around for two whole hours, Shayla wound up right back at Club XTC.

When she entered the strip club, Romeo was posted at the bar chopping it up with one of his boys. That time the club was jam packed since he'd paid a few local celebs to make guest appearances. The entire place reeked of pungent marijuana and perfume. It was the ideal T&A man cave.

Nausea washed over Shayla as she thought about dating a man who owned a strip club—or better yet having a child by one. However, this was her first pregnancy, and she didn't want to make decisions without Romeo knowing first. She owed him that much.

"Can I talk to you for a minute," Shayla asked in a surprisingly calm tone. Lately she'd been hormonal but that was to be expected.

Placing his drink on the counter, Romeo took Shayla by the hand and led her to his office. Once inside, he closed the door so they could have some peace and privacy.

"I—"

"Let—"

Romeo and Shayla stopped after realizing they were trying to speak at the same time. "You go first," she urged, wanting to stall for as long as possible.

“First, I wanna apologize for snappin’ like dat earlier,” Romeo said. “You ain’t deserve that.”

Shayla hesitated with a response. After what felt like an eternity, she finally blurted out, “I’m pregnant.”

There was a long uncomfortable pause in the room after Shayla’s unexpected revelation. Grabbing the blunt behind his ear, Romeo fired it up and took a few pulls.

“I didn’t come here for sympathy or support,” she continued. “I didn’t even come here to ask you for money. I just thought you deserved to know…before I make the appointment and all—”

“Hol’ up. Hol’ up. What appointment?”

“What appointment you think?” Shayla retorted.

“Damn. A nigga can’t get a say in this shit?” Romeo asked.

“To say what? It’s obvious you ain’t ready to be a father! How would you support us?” Shayla hounded. “Off drug money? That is what you do, right?” she patiently waited for a response to see if her guess was accurate. Shayla wasn’t surprised when she didn’t get one. “I’m not clueless. And you’re not either,” she said. “We come from two different worlds. Us being together is just a recipe for disaster…”

Romeo didn't speak as he put out his blunt and slowly approached Shayla. She was still kicking that same old bullshit when he pulled her towards him and held her. "I ain't tryin' to hear all dat. 'Cuz I don't think that's true. And deep down inside you don't either."

For a split second, Shayla lowered her guards. "I don't wanna get hurt, Romeo."

He didn't bother rushing to put her mind at ease. He'd never been the type to sell dreams. But he was definitely was willing to try and earn her trust. No woman had ever carried Romeo's seed before. And as crazy as it sounded, it was probably just what he needed to calm his feral ass down.

Instead of feeding Shayla some bull, Romeo leaned down and kissed her. Day by day, he planned on breaking down her doubts and barriers. Romeo would show her he was a real nigga with his actions.

26

Three Weeks Later

"How you like it?" Romeo asked, walking hand-in-hand with Shayla. Their footsteps echoed off the polished concrete floors of a beautiful corner-unit condo. The 11-foot floor to ceiling windows overlooked the entire Midtown.

Shayla looked like a high school girl going to her first prom, she was so excited. "I love it!" she exclaimed. Jumping up on Romeo, she wrapped her legs around him and kissed him passionately.

In spite of what her mother and ex-boyfriend thought, Shayla was taking a chance on Romeo. And she was taking an even bigger chance by keeping the baby. Though the gamble was risky, Shayla believed Romeo was worth it. She only hoped in the end, he didn't turn out acting like Cool. Speaking of him, she hadn't talked to her girl K in a minute. Regardless of their differences, Shayla hoped her life was going as well as hers.

***

"Mothafucka, what is this?!" Kim snapped.

Standing in the doorway of their bedroom, she held up a $255 Marcelo Burlon t-shirt.

"What is it?" Cool asked, squinting his eyes. He had his feet propped up on velvet pillows while watching TV—like he wasn't the biggest rat in town.

Kimberlyn wasted no time flicking the bedroom light switch on so Cool could see the lipstick print. "This shit!" she screamed. Tears pooled in her eyes as she confronted him. As foolish as it was, she'd given him a second chance and he had let her down. Apparently, old habits die hard.

When Cool didn't respond fast enough, Kim continued with her rant. "I LET YO' ASS BACK IN!"

"Calm da fuck down!" he barked. "You trippin' over dat old ass shirt. That stain could've been there! Dat don't mean I'm fuckin' around—"

Kimberlyn tossed the shirt and held her hand out. "Then let me see your phone," she demanded.

"Nah, you don't need to—"

"Let me see the fucking phone!" Kim yelled, running to the nightstand.

In the blink of an eye, Cool jumped out the bed and grabbed her by the throat. "Bitch, chill wit' all dat shit," he said before releasing her.

"I hope you had that bitch smuggling in yo' dope too!" Kim cried. "You always gon' be the same dog ass nigga. I been a real bitch since day one, and this is how you do me?"

"You doin' it to yourself," Cool said nonchalantly. "I ain't fucked around with nobody since we been back together." The fib came faster than a premature ejaculator. Unbeknownst to Kim, he'd still been hanging tough with Ava. The two had gotten so close that she even confided in him about her business. At first, Cool had only been fucking with her for the pussy, but after a while he became more interested in her organization.

Finessing Ava at all costs, Cool stuck around merely to learn the ins and outs. He kept her high most times so that she wouldn't keep up with the shit she said. Cool had even gathered that Kim's side nigga was Ava's business partner. Supposedly, she was in love with motherfucker; Cool didn't give a damn. He only wanted the empire she'd built. And he was willing to do whatever slime ass shit he had to in order to get it.

"Mothafucka, you got mo' lies to tell than a nigga in jail!" Kim spat. "If you ain't got shit to worry about, let me see your phone."

"First off, back the fuck up out my face like I'm some soft ass nigga. I'm him. Not them. Act like you know me."

Heeding his warning, Kimberlyn did as she was told. But she refused to let up on her verbal assaults. "I want you out of my damn house! Like right now, Cool."

Plopping down on the edge of the bed, he waved her off. “Fuck outta here. I ain’t goin’ nowhere.”

Cool had no consideration for her request when he pulled a tiny baggie out the nightstand’s drawer. Dumping the fine powder on the surface, he knelt down and snorted a generous amount.

Cool wasn’t tripping over the fact that he had a drug test in a couple weeks. He knew a few tricks of his own to get past that.

“So you gon’ sit here and act like you don’t hear me?” Kimberlyn asked in a calm tone. “Don’t make me call twelve on your ass, Cool.”

Cool chuckled, unfazed by her warning. Kim wasn’t crazy so he was the least bit bothered. “Nah. Call dat nigga you been fuckin’ while I was down the road.”

“Maybe I will,” she said, folding her arms.

Cool didn’t like hearing that shit. Standing to his feet, he towered over Kim by several inches. “Fuck you just say to me?” he asked through clenched teeth.

For years, Cool had been stepping out on Kimberlyn. Knowing that she was doing the same while he was imprisoned cut deep. He’d finally gotten a dose of his own medicine, and it left a bitter taste in his mouth.

Cool had already promised himself that when he crossed paths with Desmond he would kill him. In his mind, Kimberlyn was his property. Back when he met her, she was an average, simple-minded young girl. Cool had groomed her, taught her, and showed her the finer things in life. He'd even gone out his way to save her ungrateful ass aunt from homelessness. Now Kimberlyn was standing there acting like a nigga had never done anything for her. Favoring some other motherfucker like he was more important than him.

"Bitch, what the fuck you just say?!"

Suddenly, Kim regretted talking like she couldn't get touched. She was out of line and she knew it. "Cool, I—I didn't—"

Unfortunately, her explanation came a little too late.

Out of nowhere, Cool yanked Kimberlyn up by her hair and dragged her towards the hallway bathroom. "Dat new dick must've gave ya ass amnesia 'cuz you obviously don't know who you fuckin' wit'!"

"COOL, LET ME GO!" Kimberlyn screamed. She tried to pry her hair from his hands, but his vice grip was firm. Against her will, Kim was unmercifully dragged to the toilet.

Upon hearing her niece's cries, Rita quickly rushed to the hallway. She'd had a bad feeling about Cool moving back in since day one. She had even gone out her way to avoid him since he'd been back. It was obvious her doubts weren't just paranoia. Christopher "Cool" Williams was the devil reincarnated.

"LET GO OF MY HAIR!" Kimberlyn hollered. "Cool, stop—"

Kim's statement was cut short after her head was dunked inside the toilet bowl. Sadly, the last person who used it had forgotten to flush. Kimberlyn's arms flailed wildly as she fought to breathe. Her heart hammered rapidly in her chest from fear and adrenaline.

"You wanna call dat nigga—you wanna fuck dat nigga?! Where he at now? Huh?!"

Coughing and choking on the salty liquid, Kim tried her hardest to fight back. Death loomed overhead, but she would be damned if she left easily. Unluckily for her, Cool bench pressed 250 lbs. effortlessly. Kim's slapping and clawing proved useless as he continued to drown her.

Gritting his teeth, there was a menacing look in Cool's eyes. As usual, drugs and jealousy had him going off the deep end. This time, however, he'd gone too far.

Oh my God. He's really gonna kill me this time, Kim's brain registered.

"Son of a bitch! Get off her!" Rita screamed, punching at Cool's back.

In one fluid motion, Cool shoved the hell out the older woman. Losing her balance, Rita stumbled and fell into a nearby wall. The impact instantly shattered her skull, creating a large gash in the back of her head. She was dead before she even dropped.

Cool watched Rita slump to the floor at an awkward angle. Suddenly, his entire life flashed before his eyes as he thought about the jury throwing the book at him. "Shit…," Cool muttered.

"RITA?!" Kim screamed. Face and hair soaked with urine, she hurried over to her motionless aunt and reached for a pulse. When she didn't feel one, she looked up at Cool teary-eyed. "*What did you do*? WHAT DID YOU FUCKING DO?"

Cool looked like a deer caught in headlights as he stood there mouth agape, paralyzed by his own actions. Unfortunately, he didn't realize how strong he was. Now that major mistake would cost him his freedom. Not even Seth could get him out of that shit.

Cradling Rita's head in her arms, Kimberlyn gently rocked back and forth. "What did you do?" she asked repeatedly. Tears streamed down her cheeks and dripped onto the bloodstained tile.

"Mommy?" Jordan asked in a shaky tone. His tiny eyes shot open in fear after seeing his lifeless aunt sprawled out.

"No. Come here, Jordan," Cool said, reaching for him.

"Don't you fucking touch my son!" Kimberlyn screamed. Fear shook her entire body at the sight of him. She felt like she didn't even know Cool at that moment. He was an animal.

"He don't need to see this shit, K!"

"GET AWAY FROM US!"

Cool looked from Kim to Rita to his son. "Fuck!" he yelled, leaving the room. He knew without a doubt that he'd fucked up majorly. Before leaving, he punched a second hole in the wall and trashed the foyer. The future wasn't looking too bright for Cool, and he couldn't accept it.

27

"Congratulations. You're five weeks pregnant with an estimated due date of August 15th," the ultrasound tech told Romeo and Shayla. She looked more excited than Shayla did, but she still had her reservations.

Motherhood was not something she had prepared herself for. But if Romeo believed they had what it took and could make it worth, she was with it. After all, he had yet to give her any real doubts.

Squeezing Shayla's hand gently, Romeo relished the thought of being a daddy. The streets and the hustle were momentarily placed on the backburner. Nothing was more important to him than being there for Shayla.

Romeo's upbringing had been rocky, and he didn't want that for his child. He certainly wasn't an advocate of abortion. And while commitment wasn't something he was skilled at, Romeo didn't think it was impossible to learn to be.

Shayla had already proved she was worth it, so that was the least he could do. She'd weaseled her way into his heart regardless of how stubborn he acted. And she was patient through the rough transition. As a reward, Romeo moved her up out her parents' crib.

"When will we know what we havin'?" he asked the tech. Secretly, he was hoping for a son.

"Around eighteen to twenty weeks," she told them.

Romeo had a slew of other questions but his cellphone rang unexpectedly. Shayla instantly tensed up. This was their first ultrasound and she hated to share the special moment with someone else.

Staring at the screen, Romeo debated on whether or not to answer for Desmond. Truth be told, he'd even considered leaving the business altogether after finding out he was about to be a father.

Hitting the silence button, Romeo placed the phone in his pocket. He figured he'd deal with the consequences later.

Impressed that Romeo was putting her first, Shayla reached over and held his hand.

"We gon' be straight," he promised her. "Right now you number one. Everything else is just that…"

***

"Is he answering?" Ava asked. She didn't bother looking up as she continued texting Cool. She, like Romeo, had been slipping ever since someone new popped into her life. Her pot growing had even slowed down, causing the streets to run drier. Their entire organization was falling apart in front of Desmond's very eyes, and he wasn't feeling it.

Ava and Dez were at the warehouse waiting to unload when Romeo was nowhere to be found. Desmond had no idea about Romeo's good news. All he knew was that his boy had been ducking and dodging him lately. "Hell nah. Mufucka actin' like we ain't got work to do."

Over the last couple weeks, Desmond had been more strained than ever. Kimberlyn was no longer fucking with him and Dana was making his life a living hell. To make matters worse, Romeo had gone AWOL which was totally unlike him.

"Who you textin'?" Desmond asked, his tone laced with irritation.

"No one," Ava smiled, putting her phone away.

"Good. Then help me unload this shit."

***

Rita's memorial service was held at a small funeral home that contained no more than six people. Most of them were neighbors and Kimberlyn's peers. Their family had always been small so she didn't expect much. However, she was overjoyed that Shayla had showed up. In spite of their argument, it was nice to know she could put their differences aside to show support.

"How you holding up?" Shayla asked, pulling her girl into a hug.

"Holding," Kim sniffled.

Hanging onto her friend tightly, Shayla tried to take some of the weight off Kim's shoulders. She hated that she'd stayed away; and she promised herself that she would never let them fall apart and remain angry.

"K, I am so sorry about—"

"Don't even worry about it. It doesn't even matter," Kim waved her off. "I'm just happy you're here. That means more than any apology or explanation. I love you, boo."

"Love you too."

"So has there been any word from Cool?"

Kimberlyn sniffled and wiped her nose. "Nope. The police haven't been able to track him down. But they have someone on patrol circling the house every so often."

"You're more than welcome to stay with me. I have more than enough space for you and Jordan—"

"No, I'm good," Kimberlyn assured her. "Thanks though, girl. I know you got my back."

"Always," Shayla said, hugging her again.

While holding onto Shayla, Kimberlyn noticed a familiar face walk inside the funeral home. It had been a little while since the two saw each other, and she couldn't deny that she missed him like crazy. Regardless of the drama he brought her way, Desmond had left a powerful impression on her. One that made getting over him incredibly difficult.

"I'ma hit you up later, okay," Kimberlyn promised Shayla.

"Alright. And please let me know if you need anything."

After bidding her friend farewell, Kimberlyn slowly made her way to Desmond. He looked sharp in a crisp black Dolce and Gabbana suit. There wasn't a piece of lint in sight, and his light stubble only added to his appeal.

When Kimberlyn finally reached him she didn't bother speaking, apologizing, or attempting to address their last encounter. Pushing the past to the side, she wrapped her arms around Desmond and held him close.

28

One Week Later

"Fuck you been at, blood?" Desmond asked. He was going over numbers when Romeo traipsed into the warehouse's office. Heading towards the safe, he prepared to collect his dues.

"Handlin' business," Romeo answered nonchalantly. He didn't feel like explaining himself or hearing a lecture even though he knew one was coming. Romeo had been out of commission too long for it not to go addressed.

Instead of hounding him with questions, Desmond laughed and shook his head.

"What's so funny?" Romeo asked, looking over his shoulder.

"Nothin' man. It's just…I thought you said you were handlin' business. Nigga, you been MIA all month. Yo' ass ain't even been makin' drop offs like you 'posed to. But you got'cha greedy ass hands in the cookie jar—"

"Speak yo' fuckin' mind," Romeo challenged him.

Desmond hopped out his stool so fast that it toppled to the floor. "Oh, I am, my nigga! Me and Ava been bustin' our asses while you been out playin' house—"

"Look, if it's 'bout da money, keep my share 'cuz. It ain't 'een dat serious, dawg." With that said, Romeo attempted to walk around Desmond but he jumped in his face, stopping him.

"Dat's da fuckin' problem, homie! Ain't shit serious to you lately. If I ain't know any better I'd think you was flakin' on a nigga—"

"Man, get da fuck out my face. I ain't finna ask you twice," Romeo said. It took everything in him not to drop Desmond. The fact that they were friends was the only ammunition he had.

Desmond looked Romeo up and down and blew a raspberry. "You ain't hungry, blood," he said. "If you put half as much in da craft as what'chu put in chasin' ass, we'd be lookin' at some better numbers."

"Man, fuck dem numbers. Fuck this gig. And fuck you!" Romeo sneered. "I can't take none of this shit wit' me when I die. Nigga, I just found out I'm havin' a baby. I can give a fuck about meetin' yo quota. Keep dem pennies, blood. I ain't ever had a problem gettin' it. Matter fact, I planned on droppin' out soon anyway."

Desmond's jaw practically hit the floor after hearing that news. Never in his life had he heard Romeo say he wanted to give up a life of crime. Since the sand box days all they'd ever talked about was getting money together. Pink Dragon was their way out the hood…and now Romeo was saying he wanted to give it all up to be a father.

"Hol' up, dawg. Fuck you mean you droppin' out?" Desmond asked. He didn't even stop to congratulate his boy. All he cared about was the money he'd be potentially missing out on without his partner. Romeo knew a bunch of heavyweights in the streets, and he was the mouth behind the operation. Where Desmond lacked in some fields, Romeo picked up the slack. They'd always been a team. One wouldn't win without the other, and if one failed they both did. "You ain't gon' stand in my face and tell me you throwin' all dis shit away. Our blood, sweat, and tears—"

"It ain't yo' call, bruh," Romeo interrupted. "Shit, no offense, but da last thing I want is me and Shayla to end up like you and Dana. I'ma be there for mines."

Romeo's words cut deep, and he instantly thought about Destiny. Suddenly, his compassion turned to hatred.

"Man, you a ole' mark ass nigga!" Desmond yelled, shoving Romeo forcefully.

Acting on instinct, Romeo threw a devastating punch that connected with Desmond's jaw. Together the two tussled in the office of their warehouse, knocking over furniture and decorative items.

Lifting him off his feet, Desmond slammed Romeo onto the nearby oak desk before delivering a couple body shots.

Romeo ate those harsh blows before hitting Desmond with a violent right jab. The force was so powerful that it sent him stumbling backwards.

As soon as he regained his footing, Desmond made a move towards Romeo. But his friend was much faster on the draw.

Snatching out his chrome tool, Romeo pointed the barrel directly at Desmond. He had no intentions on pulling the trigger. He just wanted Dez to fall the fuck back before he seriously hurt him.

"Like that?" Desmond asked in disbelief. "You'd pull a strap on me though?"

Romeo slowly put away his burner. A $500 Givenchy tee was now ripped and ruined. "Man, ain't nobody finna shoot yo' ass. Just cut me my last check and keep it pushin', bruh. My ship'll sail with or without ya ass."

***

BOOM!

BOOM!

BOOM!

Desmond pounded on the huge wooden doors to Ava's mansion as he impatiently waited for her to answer. He'd driven so erratically to her house that he'd almost gotten in two car wrecks.

After what felt like an eternity, Ava finally opened the door wearing nothing but a white terry cloth towel. Her skin was still damp and her hair was wet. It was obvious she'd just gotten out the shower when Desmond decided to show up uninvited.

"Hey, what's up?" Ava greeted with a confused expression. It wasn't like him to pop up unannounced. Luckily, she didn't have company.

Desmond rudely barged inside and went on a rampage. "Man, can you believe this mufucka?!" he yelled at no one in particular. "Bargin' up in the office talkin' 'bout he droppin' out! Man, this fool trippin'! He fuckin' losin' it, man!"

"Who are you talking about?" Ava asked, clearly perplexed.

"First, Dana's crazy bullshit, then da mess with Kim, now Romeo—"

"I'm in love with you," Ava blurted out.

Desmond ceased his tirade long enough to turn and look at her. He wasn't expecting to hear her say that. Lately, it seemed like everyone was dropping bombs on him. Yet that one had totally caught him off guard.

For several seconds, Desmond stalled with a response. In the end, all he could come up with was, "How long?"

Ava smiled bashfully before running a hand through her long hair. "Since the first time I ever saw you," she answered honestly.

There was a long uncomfortable silence as the two stared at each other. Desmond was at a total loss for words. Up until then, he'd always looked at Ava like a little sister. Now she was telling him that she had always possessed feelings for him. His luck with women was ultimately his curse.

"Say something…," Ava whispered.

Desmond chuckled nervously before running a hand over his waves. "I…What do you want me to say?"

Ava offered a flirtatious smile before unloosening her towel. In silence, Desmond watched as it dropped loosely around her ankles.

Immediately, his eyes took in everything his best friend had to show. Ava's perky C-cup breasts were full and supple. Her kitty was shaved low, and the sight of it alone made Desmond's mouth water.

"The real question is…what are you gonna do?"

29

Desmond abandoned all morals when he walked up to Ava and kissed her. If he didn't get the pussy, he'd feel like a pussy later on. Besides, a real nigga would fuck a friend.

Wrapping her toned arms and legs around Desmond, Ava eagerly submitted. Any possible consequences seemed nonexistent as he carried her to the master bedroom. Gently placing her down on the mattress, Desmond's head screamed no while the other said yes.

Ava anxiously undid his jeans in excitement. After snatching them down his athletic legs, she slipped his curved 10-inch dick inside her mouth.

"*Mmm*," Desmond moaned. Grabbing a handful of her hair, he guided Ava's head up and down his shaft.

She sucked his dick with so much intensity and devotion. Almost as if she didn't want another bitch to matter.

When Desmond could no longer stand the foreplay, he flipped Ava over onto her stomach. "Put dat ass up," he demanded.

Desmond didn't bother returning the oral pleasure as he spat in his palm. Lathering his mandingo, he slid deep inside Ava. Grabbing a fistful of her locks, he pounded into her like he hated her ass. And in a way he did. Deep down inside, Desmond didn't want to take shit there, but she made it hard for a nigga to refuse.

Anger and resentment brewed in Desmond's heart as he fucked harder. Gripping the bed sheets, Ava tried her best to take the aggressive strokes. "*Aaaah*, shit!" she yelped. "Slow down, Dez."

"You wanted the D, now take it," he said in total disregard.

Handling Ava like a ragdoll, Desmond flipped her over onto her back. "Spread dem legs."

When he slid inside, Ava leaned up to kiss him but he turned his head away. There was a total disconnection.

So many thoughts ran through Desmond's mind as he pounded into Ava. She had no idea he'd be taking his frustrations out on her after offering herself to him.

Wrapping a hand around her slender throat, Desmond fucked Ava into euphoria. With her legs quivering, she secreted all over him. Her orgasm was so powerful that it sent her eyes rolling to the back of her head.

After pumping Ava a few more good times, Desmond snatched out and skeeted on her thigh. The moment he collapsed beside her he felt instant regret. As incredible as the hate sex was, it also left

Desmond feeling numb on the inside. His heart wasn't with Ava.

So why I fuck her?

Ava rolled over so she could look at Desmond. He was unusually quiet, and she knew something was up. "How do you feel…?" she asked timidly.

Ava knew how much Desmond valued their friendship; and she hoped the sex wouldn't complicate things. But she also knew if she didn't take a chance by telling him how she felt, she'd always wonder what if.

Ava waited on pins and needles for a response. However, she was totally crushed when Desmond said, "I feel like I love somebody else…"

Ava's entire world came crushing down after his statement. As a matter of fact, it felt like a slap in the face. She'd tossed all her cards on the table by proclaiming her love—and now he was telling her she wasn't good enough for him.

"Are you serious?" Ava asked, sitting up in bed. "I finally open up to you and that's how you do me—"

"I didn't ask you to. Quite frankly, you could've kept it to yaself if you ain't want your feelings hurt." Desmond was heartless with his response, but nonetheless real. Of course, Ava didn't want to hear that shit.

"Fuck you, Desmond! Get the fuck out my bed!"

"Really?"

"I'm not playing! Get the fuck out!"

Ava's entire face was beet red with embarrassment and anger. She'd never felt so humiliated and betrayed. For years, Ava had imagined him declaring his love back, but apparently he wasn't feeling her the way she was him. That realization hurt like hell.

"What the hell is yo' problem?!"

"You are!" Ava cried. "I told you that I loved you! And in turn you fucked me like I was some prostitute before telling me you have feelings for another bitch! You could've kept that shit!"

"And you could've kept that towel on," Desmond retaliated. "But you didn't. Just like I didn't promise I'd fall in love with yo' ass after we fucked."

If there was a gun within reach, Ava would've shot his ass point blank. They were supposed to be friends, but Desmond was treating her like she was one of his jump offs.

Tossing a pillow at his head, Ava screamed for him to leave. Desmond couldn't dress fast enough. "Look, it's nothin' personal. Hit me up when you get out yo' feelings," he said on his way out.

After hearing the front door close, Ava hopped out her bed and began trashing the room. She knocked over and broke anything she could get her hands on. Hot tears streamed down her cheeks when she pushed her LED TV over.

The drugs coupled with a wounded pride had Ava spazzing out. "Fuck him!" she screamed. "I hate him! I hate him! I hate his ass!"

After tuckering herself out, Ava dropped onto the floor in the middle of her room. She was so upset and hurt that all she wanted to do was make Desmond suffer the same way she was.

Suddenly, an idea popped into Ava's mind. Grabbing her iPhone she dialed a dear friend's number. When he answered on the fourth ring, she wasted no time, "I think I gotta proposition for you."

30

That evening, Shayla and Romeo enjoyed a candlelit dinner at *Bacchanalia*, an Italian 4-star restaurant in the heart of midtown. With a quiet and modern ambience, delicious food, and hospitable staff, it was a gem to experience. However, Shayla's only issue was the fact that Dexter and Nina were coincidentally dining there as well.

Romeo didn't miss the irritation on Shayla's face. But he would be damned if he allowed an ex to ruin his evening—especially when he had a big surprise in store.

"Man, fuck dat clown. You with yo' nigga. He irrelevant," Romeo said. Every so often he noticed her glance in Dexter's direction and it was starting to annoy him.

"I know, I know," Shayla agreed. "But you'd think outta all the restaurants in Atlanta he could go eat somewhere else."

"Shayla…? You wanna invite the mufucka over to join us?"

Shayla looked repulsed. "No! Of course not."

"Aight then. Drop it. They asses ain't fazed by us so why you sweatin' him?"

Shayla could tell she was irritating Romeo so she decided to chill. He'd gone out his way to make reservations and she didn't want to let a small misfortune ruin his effort.

"Aye, I got'chu somethin'," Romeo said, changing his tone.

Shayla's eyes instantly lit up when he placed a navy suede box on the table. "What is it?" she asked excitedly. Romeo had been spoiling her nonstop since they'd been kicking it, and the presents were only getting better.

No one knew it, but there was once a time when Shayla was envious of the way Cool spoiled Kim. Now it was her time to shine.

"Open it," Romeo urged.

Shayla took her time lifting the lid. A sharp gasp instantly escaped her lips at the sight of a sparkling 10 ct. ring. "Oh, my…Romeo—I—what is this?" she stuttered. Shayla was flabbergasted at the sight of the ring. She had no idea what it meant.

Romeo chuckled lightly. "What'chu think it is? I'm tryin' to do right with you," he told her. "Wassup? You wit' it or not?"

Shayla's smile slowly vanished. Romeo's delivery was all wrong, and it was far too early. She also felt like he was asking out of obligation. On top of it all, the setting was horrible considering Dexter was seven feet away. "I'm…uh…" Shayla paused as she carefully thought about her response. "I'm gonna put the ring on…but I don't know if it's quite a yes yet…"

Romeo immediately looked offended. He wasn't used to women turning him away. It took a lot of courage for him to pop the big question, and she didn't even want to give him an honest answer. "Nah, gimme my mufuckin' ring back then. It don't work like that," he said.

"Why do I have to give it back? I didn't say no. I just don't think you're fully ready for something like this."

"Why can't I be?"

"You barely can keep your eyes off waitresses still. But you ready to spend a life with me? Boy, stop it."

Suddenly, Romeo regretted the decision to give up his hustle for Shayla. It was obvious that she wasn't taking a nigga seriously. "You know what? I done lost my appetite," he said. "On some real shit, I'm ready to dip."

Although she wasn't prepared to leave, Shayla did as he asked. Romeo could be so petty when he didn't get his way, and that was something she was unsure if she could get over. As they prepared to leave, Dexter glanced over at their section. Shayla half-expected him to do or say something. Yet she wasn't surprised when he reached over and placed his hand over Nina's. After finding out Shayla was having another nigga's baby, Dexter had to force himself to move on.

"You see the way you're acting?" Shayla said on their way out. "That right there lets me know you ain't ready."

"Man, whatever. Just get in the fuckin' car."

Shayla quickly stopped in her tracks. She was pissed that Romeo was even behaving so childishly. "I'm straight. I'll catch a cab," she told him, walking in the opposite direction.

"Shayla, get in the car, man! I ain't finna play these baby games."

Shayla ignored Romeo as she walked away while fishing through her purse for her cell. When it was obvious that she wouldn't conform, Romeo hopped in his Porsche and skirted off. No bitch was worth chasing in his opinion. If Shayla wanted to play head games she'd have to solo. He had already given her all of him, and if she couldn't see the sincerity it wasn't worth it anyway.

***

Kim peered out her large bay window for the seventh time that evening. Strangely, she hadn't seen a cop drive past in three hours. Usually, they were consistent but it was obvious they'd gotten lax.

Kimberlyn had put Jordan to bed an hour ago, and while he slept soundlessly she kept an alert. After Rita's passing and rekindling with Desmond, he had offered to move her in but she didn't want the messiness. Instead, she opted to take their time with each other and see where things went.

There was no denying the chemistry with Desmond. Kimberlyn just wasn't ready to jump back in something so quickly—especially while she was vulnerable.

"Where are these motherfuckers?" she asked herself. Chalking their absence up to a temporary break, Kim headed back to the living room. She was halfway there when she heard a knock on her front door.

Kimberlyn instantly froze in place. She knew it was trouble without even having to look through the peephole.

"Kimmy, it's me...," Cool called out. "Listen, I know I fucked up...but I need you. Open the door fuh me."

Though he sounded sincere and apologetic, Kim would be a fool to let him back in. He had caused more than enough grief to last a lifetime. Padding barefoot to the door, she pressed her body against it and spoke. "Cool...The police are doing rounds every hour looking for you," Kim began. "If I were you, I'd leave."

"I can't leave without you," he told her.

There was a long period of silence afterwards.

Kim longed to open the door and hold him, but there was also a part of her that was scared of him. And love couldn't co-exist with fear.

Cool sniffled and wiped his nose. He was high out his mind at that very moment, but it was the only way he could get the courage to visit Kim. "Look, bay…I'm plannin' somethin' big tonight. Somethin' that could set me straight for a lil' while."

Kimberlyn remained silent as she listened to him.

"When I'm done, I wanna take you and Jordan and get the fuck up outta here," Cool said. "I need to get ghost ASAP…but I can't bounce without my fam. And in spite of all da shit dat happened between us, you always gon' be dat, K. You the mother of my son, yo."

Tears streamed down Kimberlyn's cheeks. Even with all the chaos he had caused, there was no denying she still loved Cool. Letting him go permanently hurt like hell. But ultimately, time healed all wounds.

"I'm sorry, Cool. But if you don't leave I'm calling the police."

Angered by her stubbornness, he instantly went off the deep end. “Open this mothafuckin’ door, Kim!”

Flinching at his thunderous tone, she quickly backed away from the door.

“OPEN THIS FUCKIN’ DOOR!”

BOOM!

BOOM!

BOOM!

31

Desmond had been driving around the last half an hour clearing his mind when Kimberlyn called. Turning the music down to his Jeezy CD, he answered immediately. "Wassup? Everything good?"

Desmond could barely make out what Kim was saying since she was talking so frantically. But at the mention of Cool's name, he did an automatic U-turn in the road and headed her way.

Halfway there, his cellphone rang again. Thinking it was Kimberlyn calling back, Desmond answered without even looking at the caller ID.

"Yo."

"Hey, babe. You busy?"

Desmond growled in frustration. "Not right now, Dana."

"*Then when*?" she whined.

"Fuck off, Dana! Now ain't the time, man!"

"So it's like that?" she asked. "You really gon' toss me to the side while you entertain some other hoe? I'm fam, remember?"

"You the mother of my chill, Dana. That's it…"

Dana paused as she allowed Desmond's hurtful words to sink in. "So I ain't yo' bitch no more?"

CLICK!

Desmond didn't have time to go back and forth with his baby mama. He had a situation to tend to that was much more important. It took him less than ten minutes to pull up on Kimberlyn. As expected, he found Cool's crazy ass banging on the front door like *Fred Flintstone*.

This nigga.

Desmond shook his head in disgust at the sight of it all. He was a real fucking problem that Dez was tempted to get rid of. Had it not been for Cool being Kim's baby daddy, he would've had his ass clapped, end of story.

Inside, Kimberlyn and Jordan were locked in his bedroom with a loaded gun. She had called Desmond instead of the police, because as much as she hated Cool she still didn't want to see him rot. Kim was hoping Desmond could talk him down without things escalating to violence.

After parking his car, Desmond killed the engine and hopped out. He thought about grabbing his burner, but figured it was best not to. "Aye, bruh? Wassup?" Desmond asked, walking up on Cool.

At the sound of his voice, Cool slowly turned around to face Desmond. Just the sight of the nigga who'd been fucking his baby mama made his skin crawl.

Cool laughed softly before shaking his head. "This bitch really called this nigga though," he said to himself. "I rather she called da pigs."

"Look, I ain't tryin' to get hostile tonight, man," Desmond said in a non-confrontational tone. "Quite frankly, it ain't none of my business what'chu got goin' on. All I care about is Kimberlyn and her son. And they're in there scared right now," he explained. "So man to man, I'm askin' you to fall back. Ain't no police gotta get called, bruh. Just roll out."

All of a sudden, the front door to the house opened and out walked Kimberlyn. Now that Desmond was there she felt secure enough to exit.

Cool laughed menacingly as he looked from Kim to Desmond. His glassy eyes were a result of cocaine and LSD. "This yo' mufuckin' cavalry?" he joked, throwing shade at Dez. "Bitch, I oughta kill you and this lame ass nigga."

"Cool, just leave," Kimberlyn boldly spoke up.

"Fuck you," Cool spat. "If you wanna stay wit' this buster that's cool, but I ain't goin' nowhere without my son. And that's straight up."

"He's not your son," Kimberlyn told him.

Surprised by the news, Cool and Desmond looked up at her at the same time.

"Fuck you just say?" Cool asked through clenched teeth. Tears pooled in his eyes as his worst realization manifested. It felt as if Kimberlyn had just snatched a rug from underneath him.

"Jordan's not your son," she repeated with more authority. "He's Desmond's."

"What?" they said in unison.

Tears slipped from her eyes as she looked over at Dez. "I'm sorry," she cried. "I swear I wanted to tell you when you came back in town…but I could never find the time…"

That had been a secret that Kimberlyn planned on taking to her grave. But if Cool fucked around and got arrested that night, then he at least deserved to know.

"Cool…," Kimberlyn began. "I—"

All of a sudden, he reached in his waistband and pulled out a strap. "You mothafucka!" he yelled, aiming at Desmond.

Kimberlyn hopped off the porch and ran towards the love of her life. "*NOOOO*!" she screamed.

POP!

32

The bullet intended for Desmond, struck Kimberlyn directly in the abdomen. The shot was enough to send her falling, but luckily Dez caught her on the way down. Together, they collapsed onto the ground.

Kimberlyn was completely motionless as she lay sprawled out in his arms. Dark red blood poured from a dime-sized gunshot wound. If they didn't get her to the hospital fast, there was no doubt she'd bleed out.

"Fuck you standin' there for?! GET HELP!" Desmond screamed. Tears dropped from his eyes as he thought about the possibility of losing her. He couldn't. Not after knowing everything he knew. Not after falling in love with her a second time.

Instead of doing something to save Kimberlyn's life, Cool hopped in his car and peeled off.

***

It was 9: 12 p.m. when Dana strutted in Fulton County's Police Department. The wounds were still fresh on her neck, and she was ready to give a full testimony—even a little fabrication for good measures. Dana planned to air out everything, including the million dollar business Desmond cherished so much.

I gave his ass ample time to get it together, she thought. *Now his ass is gonna learn.*

***

Desmond's bloodstained hands trembled as he held onto his steering wheel. Twenty minutes ago, Kimberlyn had been rushed into the ER and her fate was still on verdict.

Instead of sitting around in the waiting room, Desmond decided to wait outside in his car. He always felt like people who waited in those waiting rooms were waiting on bad luck.

She's gonna make it, Desmond told himself. As bad as his nerves were, he refrained from firing up with his son in the backseat. Right now the five-year old needed him to have a clear conscience. Jordan was far too young to understand what was happening. And with Rita gone and Cool on the run, Desmond was all he had.

Suddenly, Desmond's cellphone rang. He was somewhat surprised when he saw it was Ava. "I hope she ain't on dat bullshit 'cuz now ain't the time," he said to himself.

Going against his better judgment, Desmond went ahead and answered. "What, Ava?"

"Desmond! You have to come quick! I'm so fucking!" she cried out, panic-stricken.

"Hold up. Slow down, V. What's goin' on?"

"I must've forgotten to lock up. It's the warehouse!" she exclaimed. "I think we've been robbed!"

"Fuck, V, damn, man! Look, I'm on my way!" Desmond didn't even bother disconnecting the call before tossing his phone in the passenger seat. Putting the pedal to the metal, he flew towards Old Fourth Ward District.

***

Jordan was fast asleep by the time Desmond arrived to the warehouse. Parking his car, he quickly hopped out and ran inside. Ava's whip was parked not too far so he knew she was there as well.

On his way inside, Desmond called up Romeo but got his voicemail instead.

If it ain't one thing it's another, he thought.

Desmond was totally caught off guard by the sight of Cool standing next to Ava. It didn't take his mind long to realize he'd been set up.

Desmond quickly reached for his piece, but Cool beat him to punch. "Nah, bruh. None of that," he said, smiling wickedly. "Put ya heat down and kick it over to me."

Begrudgingly, Desmond did as he was instructed. Cool had been waiting for that moment, and Ava had finally blessed him with the opportunity for payback. Unfortunately, there was nothing more dangerous than two scorned lovers.

"Damn, V. Like that, huh?" Desmond asked Ava. He couldn't believe his own girl had turned on him. She was supposed to be fam, but now she was treating him like he was her worse enemy. It wasn't even about the money. It was about her heart. And after fucking her, Desmond had stomped on it without the slightest consideration. Sadly, he would have to pay for the rejection with his life.

"I made you a millionaire," Ava reminded him. "And in turn you treated me like shit. So like you told me earlier…It's nothing personal…" The devilish smirk on her face would forever haunt Desmond. He barely recognized her at that very moment.

Desmond looked over at Cool in disgust. Had it not been for the gun he was holding, he would've broken the motherfucker's jaw. "You just shot ya girl, bruh. She in da hospital right now fightin' for her life." Desmond's voice trembled with emotion as he filled Cool in. He couldn't believe the nigga cared more about him than his own girl.

"Fuck that bitch," Cool said, cocking the loaded gun. "She made her choice…now I'm makin' mine…"

POP!

33

Shayla wasn't surprised when she found Romeo's car parked at Club XTC. It seemed like whenever they fell out he went back to doing the same old shit. She wanted to be mad at him, but she knew if they had to make it work they had to communicate first.

Inside, Shayla found Romeo chilling with a colorful section of girls. It was so obvious they missed their handsome boss. Eminem's "*Superman*" poured through the club's speakers. Shayla felt depressed just being in there, and she wished he'd just come home.

Jealousy coursed through her blood as she approached Romeo. She was so fed up with the back and forth games. *Either he wants me or not*, she told herself.

"Romeo, I need to talk to you," Shayla said once she reached him.

"I'm busy," Romeo said, puffing on a blunt. He figured if he dissed Shayla she'd take the hint but she didn't. Unlike most women he dated, she didn't back down easily. That was the main reason they bumped heads so often.

"You mean to tell me the mother of your child can't get two minutes?" Shayla asked, propping a hand on her hip.

"*If* da lil' mufucka even mine," Romeo added cynically. He was really reaching and he knew it. His comment cut deep and Shayla quickly walked off in anger.

The nerve of this nigga to think I'm trying to get over on his ass.

Her heels clicked against the pavement as she walked across the lot. She couldn't believe she'd foolishly thought Romeo would change. Just as she reached in her purse for her car keys, her cellphone chimed indicating a text.

Tears blurred Shayla's vision as she pulled her iPhone out and attempted to read it. The text message was from Dexter:

I tried to get over u…but I hated seeing you wit dat mufucka tonite. He ain't for u and u know it babe. I wanna make it work still with us. I won't forgive myself for letting you go, Shay. Hit me back.

"Is it a full moon or something," Shayla muttered, tossing her phone in her bag. Dexter was the last person she wanted to be bothered with.

Hitting the automatic door unlock button, Shayla prepared to climb inside her Benz—Suddenly, a strong pair of arms snatched her up from behind. Placing a chloroform-soaked rag over her mouth, her captor quickly rendered her unconscious. The car keys uncontrollably slipped from her fingers as her entire body went limp.

Shayla barely had a chance to put up a fight before she was tossed inside a dark trunk.

Meanwhile inside the club, it didn't take Romeo long to regret what he'd said. Fanning off his groupies, he ran outside to see if Shayla was still there. *Damn, this girl got me tripping*, he told himself. No woman had ever gotten under skin like her. One minute Romeo couldn't stand her ass, and the next he couldn't stand being away. Regardless of their differences though, it was no doubt that he loved Shayla. If he didn't, he surely wouldn't have gone after her stubborn ass.

Strangely, when Romeo went outside, Shayla was nowhere in sight despite her car still parked.

"The fuck?"

Suspicions on high alert, Romeo reached for his piece and looked around frantically. Something didn't feel right in the atmosphere. After noticing a small piece of paper under Shayla's windshield wiper, Romeo jogged over to see what it was.

Hastily scribbled on the note was a simple message: *You got somethin' we want, now we got somethin' you want.*

After hearing tires screeching, Romeo looked up and noticed a boxed Chevy pulling out the lot. His heart instantly sank to the pit of his stomach after learning Shayla's fate. It didn't take long to realize his girl had been kidnapped for ransom. His worse fear had come to life.

"SHAYLA!" Romeo screamed. The soles of his Timberlands, scraped the pavement as he took off after the car. "*SHAYLA*?!"

TO BE CONTINUED…

ABOUT THE AUTHOR

Jade Jones discovered her passion for creative writing in elementary school. Born in 1989,she began writing poetry as an outlet. She then converted her poetry into short stories. Later on, as a teen, she led a troubled life which later resulted in her becoming a ward of the court. Jade fell in love with the art and used storytelling as a means of venting during her tumultuous times. Aging out of the system two years later, she was thrust into the dismal world of homelessness.

Desperate, and with limited income, Jade began dancing full time at the tender age of eighteen. It wasn't until Fall of 2008 when she finally caught her break after being accepted into Cleveland State University. There, she lived on campus and majored in Film and Television. Now, six years later, she flourishes from her childhood dream of becoming a bestselling author. Since then she has written the best-selling "Cameron" series and the highly-rated "Schemin'" trilogy. Quite suitably, she uses her life experiences to create captivating characters and story lines.

Jade currently resides in Atlanta, Georgia. With no children, she spends her leisure shopping and traveling. She says that seeing new faces, meeting new people, and experiencing diverse cultures fuels her creativity. The stories are generated in her heart, the craft is practiced in her mind, and she expresses her passion through ink. To learn more, visit www.jadedpublications.com

EXCERPT FROM "BACKPAGE"

1

"If you're looking for someone to take your mind off the stress, call me..."

Sweater Robinson sashayed across the bar/rooftop deck in a form-fitting leather Bodycon dress. Her cheetah print Louboutins grabbed the attention of every woman in the place, and her large, round ass grabbed the eye of every man.

The half black, half white 5"5 beauty commanded attention whenever she walked into a place. Often told that she resembled songstress Mya, Sweater had an innocent but sultry look about her that both men and women alike found irresistible.

The rhinestones glistened on Sweater's two-inch stiletto nails as she held her iPhone against her ear. Her hazel eyes scanned the crowd filled with professionals and entrepreneurs from every business field.

"Hello sweetheart," Kenyon answered in a smooth, deep tone.

"What are you wearing?" Sweater asked. Her gaze settled on a dark skinned, bald-head brother standing near the railing while nursing a Martini.

"Flesh colored dress shirt and black slacks."

A smiled tugged at the corner of Sweater's full, pouty lips. Without another word, she disconnected the call and sauntered towards Mr. Bald and Chocolate—also known as Kenyon.

Kenyon's eyes lit up the moment they saw Sweater. As expected she was everything her advertisement said she'd be and more. *She looked a bit thicker in her photos but she's still bad as hell*, he thought to himself as he spread his arms for a hug.

"Nice to finally meet you, Honey," Kenyon greeted, addressing Sweater by her fake name.

There was no way in hell she was going to broadcast her unique name to the public. As a matter of fact there was only a handful that knew her by her government. Yet she was the only one who knew the captivating story behind it.

"You look even more handsome than I imagined," Sweater lied. In her opinion, Kenyon looked more like a combination of Seal and Mike Tyson—but that didn't matter since he was one of the best cosmetic surgeons in the Atlanta metropolitan area. His pockets easily made up for his lack of good looks, and he'd been nothing short of a gentleman since the very first phone call two nights ago.

Kenyon explained that he simply needed a chaperone to make him look good for the evening, but Sweater was positive that before the night ended he'd be expecting some pussy. After all, that's what the escort section of www.backpage.com was all about.

If you weren't an undercover cop looking to make a quick bust, you were a lonely individual in desperate need of attention and companionship. To most any type of warmth was better than being cold so clients dug into their bank accounts or fished in their wallets to pay for a spectacular evening with no limitations.

"Thank you sweetie. I really appreciate that," Kenyon said. "Would you like a drink or something?" He held up his martini to indicate if she'd like the same.

Clearly he didn't know Sweater because she would never be caught dead drinking that weak ass beverage. Much like her late mother she was a heavy alcoholic that spent most of her weekends binge drinking.

"I'll pass for now," Sweater answered sweetly. "I wanna be sober and aware of everything I have planned for you tonight," she purred in his ear.

Kenyon's dick jerked awake behind the thin fabric of his dress pants, but he tried his best to compose himself. "Is that right? Well let me finish this and we can go up to the room," he said. He then turned his attention to Atlanta's mesmerizing skyline. The beautiful lights and scenery made for a breathtaking view.

Sweater joined Kenyon and took in the sight before her. In the six short years that she'd been living in Georgia she'd never seen its actual skyline from an overhead view. For two whole minutes her problems suddenly became nonexistent. Her dark past seemed irrelevant. And her insecurities seemed to disappear.

"Beautiful isn't it?" Kenyon asked, breaking the silence.

"Most definitely," Sweater agreed.

Kenyon then focused his attention on the woman whose company he was paying handsomely for. "You from Atlanta?" he asked.

"No," Sweater answered, keeping her gaze on the city's view. "I'm actually from California." The lie left her lips before she could fully think it up. She was actually born and raised in Cleveland, Ohio and hadn't visited the west coast a day in her life.

Sweater was the epitome of the phrase "habitual liar". She lied about any and everything, and was so used to doing it that she began to believe her own ridiculous fibs.

Kenyon looked surprised by her answer. "California, really? That's interesting," he nodded his head in approval.

"Yeah, I'm a west coast baby," Sweater smiled. There was a faraway look in her eyes as she reminisced on a memory that never took place. "Sometimes I can still smell the ocean," she said. "…Feel the sand in my toes…smell the palm trees. I miss the beach most of all. I can still remember my mom taking me and my sisters to Venice Beach for the first time. The sun was extra bright that day…it was one of the best days of my life."

"Sounds memorable," Kenyon said. "I've never been to California. Maybe if we get better acquainted we can go together and you could show me around. How does that sound?"

There was as much chance of that happening as it was Sweater not telling another lie before the night ended. "Okay, I'm going to hold you to that," she smiled. "Anyway it's getting a little nifty out here. Don't you agree?" Sweater rubbed her arms for good measure. It was in the late eighties but she basically needed an excuse to get Kenyon alone.

"Alright, we can leave," he agreed.

After placing the empty martini glass on a nearby table, Sweater followed Kenyon back inside the luxurious five-star hotel. He didn't bother spitting any lame ass game to let her know he wanted some since she already knew what was up.

"Here we are," Kenyon said once they reached room 1201. His hard dick strained against his pants as he envisioned all the freaky shit he planned on doing to Sweater. He hoped like hell her ad was right about her having no limitations, but if she did he didn't plan on forcing her. He may have been a freak but he was also a reputable man.

Sweater patiently waited for him to swipe his hotel keycard. Her palms began to sweat as anxiety washed over her.

"Now before we go in just know that you don't have to do anything you don't want to," Kenyon assured her. "I know you're here for me but I want you to be equally as comfortable because I won't feel comfortable if you don't."

"I understand," Sweater whispered, fidgeting with her clutch. She was a little bit nervous but she tried her best to appear calm. It was always that exact moment where her confidence melted away.

"Good."

Kenyon stepped closer to Sweater, cupped her small face in his hands, and placed a light peck on her lips. "I'm a very passionate man…just so you know…"

"I understand…"

"Good."

Kenyon then opened the door and allowed Sweater entrance before he himself stepped inside. As he prepared to close the door, a hooded figure instantly bum rushed inside the small room!

The metal door slammed against Kenyon's 5"9 inch frame, sending him crashing down onto the carpeted floor. It felt like the wind had been knocked out of him as he struggled to comprehend what had just happened.

Royalty Jackson III slammed and locked the door behind him before snatching the hood off his head. The 6"1 inch dark-brown skinned thug was extremely handsome in a rugged sense. He wore his short box fade cut and styled similar to Bishop's in the film, Juice and had the exact same swag and demeanor to match. Royalty was reckless and didn't give a fuck about anything.

"What the hell is your problem?!" Kenyon yelled, standing to his feet. However, the minute he caught sight of Royalty's Beretta he froze in place.

Suddenly, Sweater walked up from behind and snatched Kenyon's wallet out his back pocket. She then tossed it to Royalty who managed to keep his gun aimed at Kenyon as he caught it.

Kenyon turned towards Sweater with rage-filled eyes. "You bitch! You set me up!"

Sweater smiled. "Surprised? Shit like this happens all the time, boo."

With his fists clenched tightly, Kenyon took a step towards her—but quickly stopped in his tracks after hearing the sound of Royalty's gun being cocked. Hesitantly, he refocused his attention on the armed assailant.

"Aight then homeboy, this what we finna do," Royalty's strong southern accent was profound. "We 'bout to hit up da bank. We gon' make two withdrawals. One before midnight and one after. Now I want this to go smooth and simple. I ain't tryin' to hurt nobody, ya dig?"

"Fuck you!" Kenyon spat. "I'm not doing shit for you or this bitch!"

“Oh, you tough?” Royalty asked skeptically. He pulled Kenyon’s identification cards and photos out and flipped through them all the while keeping his gun aimed at Kenyon. “Well, we’ll see how tough you are when I send my folks to ya crib.” Royalty smiled revealing his gold fangs. “I see you got a beautiful wife and daughter who don’t even know you up in this spot tryin’ to get some pussy—”

“If you hurt my family, I swear to God I’ll kill you!”

Royalty rushed Kenyon, and pistol-whipped the shit out of him with the butt of his Beretta! Blood gushed from Kenyon’s nose and soaked his dress shirt. He stumbled backwards after the blow but somehow managed to keep his footing.

Royalty pulled his cellphone out and dialed a number up. He kept his intense gaze locked on Kenyon. It was important that he let him know who was in charge.

When the person on the opposite end answered, Royalty rattled off Kenyon’s address and informed them that he also had a family. After passing the info on, Royalty disconnected the call and directed his attention back to Kenyon.

“I’m runnin’ this show, bruh! Now let’s try this shit again! You gon’ make two withdrawals takin’ out da maximum limit. One before midnight and one after. The sooner you just cooperate the quicker we can get this shit done. Do you got that? ‘Cuz my patna got ya info now and I'd hate for some ugly shit to go down. Ya dig?"

Kenyon covered his bloodied nose and nodded his head in agreement.

"Sorry you had to be a victim, hon'," Sweater said. "But it's all business...never personal."

***

Fifteen minutes after walking out of the Glenn Hotel together, the trio pulled inside the empty Bank of America parking lot located on Ponce De Leon Avenue. There were fewer witnesses around and the area was somewhat low-key.

"Get out the car *slowly*—and no funny shit, aight?" Royalty stressed.

Kenyon grimaced as he held in the threats he desperately wanted to utter. As instructed, he took his time climbing out his gun metal black 2012 Mercedes Benz. Sweater followed suit, glancing around at her surroundings every so often to make sure no one was within distance.

Keeping his gun aimed on Kenyon, Royalty rounded the car, and snatched him up by the back of his collar. "Let's make this shit quick. We ain't got all fuckin' night to be bullshittin'."

Kenyon stepped in front of the ATM and stared at the bright red screen for several seconds. "I can only withdraw $100," he said.

WHAP!

The butt of Royalty's Beretta crashed down on Kenyon's skull.

"*Oomph*!" he groaned in pain, falling against the ATM machine.

"Bruh, stop fuckin' around! Ya max is 500 so who the fuck you really tryin' to fool?" Royalty asked. "I been doin' this shit longer then you prolly knew what the fuck a Backpage was. So stop bullshittin' with me!" He then checked the time on his cellphone. It was a quarter until midnight. "Ya time's windin' down. Now it's up to you if you wanna sacrifice ya family's lives over a stack. It ain't shit but a call away, man."

"Okay. Okay. Okay. I got it," Kenyon finally caved. He held onto the back of his head where a knot had quickly formed. "But I'll need my wallet to get the debit card."

My patience is really starting to grow thin with this mothafucka, Royalty thought to himself as he reached in his pocket to get the wallet—

Kenyon used that opportunity to deliver a fierce punch to Royalty's jaw. The blow was so unexpected that it sent Royalty crashing onto the ground.

Kenyon wasted no time as he took off running in the opposite direction.

"Motherfucker!" Sweater hissed. She'd witnessed the entire scene unfold.

Sweater quickly jumped into the Benz to pursue him.

By the time Royalty stood to his feet, Kenyon was already sprinting across the bank's parking lot.

Sweater snatched the gears into drive and floored the gas pedal. Like a police officer racing after a fleeing criminal, she chased down Kenyon until she was finally alongside him. After ensuring that it was enough space between them, Sweater flung open the driver's door.

BOOM!

The metal door slammed into Kenyon and he crashed onto the pavement face first after the impact. Afterward, Sweater brought the Benz to a screeching stop.

"My fucking leg," Kenyon groaned in pain, cradling his injured knee. Something told him it seemed foolish to try to run, but with fear and adrenaline coursing through his veins it was hard to think clearly.

When Royalty finally reached Kenyon, he snatched the disoriented man off the ground and dragged him towards the car's front door. "I told you not to fuck with me but I see you wanna try a nigga!" he yelled. Royalty opened the door, and placed Kenyon's right arm inside.

"No! No! No!"

WHAM!

"*AHHHHH*!" Kenyon screamed in pain after Royalty slammed the door against his forearm.

A terrible decision had now forced him to deal with the twenty-five year old's intermittent explosive disorder. After serving a few years in the military, Royalty wasn't the same man as he was when he enrolled. The doctors blamed it on posttraumatic stress disorder.

Royalty shoved the barrel of his gun inside Kenyon's mouth. "You must wanna take ya last breath tonight!" he said through clenched teeth. The fury in his eyes made him look more monster than human. "I ain't the one to fuck with," Royalty stressed. "I'll put a got damn hole in ya head right now and then murk ya folks just because." He then lowered himself to Kenyon's eye level. "And I'm not talkin' no quick and easy death. I will fuck ya wife until she begs me to kill her, and then I'll torture ya lil' girl—"

"Please, no!" Kenyon burst out in hysterical cries. Mucus oozed from his nostrils mixing in with dark red blood. "Man, I'm begging you don't hurt my family—"

"Their fate's on you," Royalty simply said. "You're doin' this shit the hard way when you should be doin' it the easy way."

Visit our website www.jadedpublications.com to grab your copy!

OTHER TITLES FROM JADED PUBLICATIONS

Cameron

What Bae Don't Know

Dope Boys and Other 4 Letter Words

Nothing New Except Someone New

Reality Check

When a Rich Thug Wants You